SOME SAILORS NEVER DIE

Monsters and Mayhem Book Three

E A COMISKEY

Scarsdale Publishing, Ltd

SP

TRADEMARK ACKNOWLEDGMENTS

Pizza Junction Café

Mick Jagger

The Eagles – "Witchy Woman"

Prince/The Artist Formerly Known As Prince (lyrics from "Kiss" by Prince)

The Weather Channel

Beaver Cleaver

Gigantor

Mr. Clean

Oscar (award)

Dan Brown

Norman Mailer's *The Fight*

Prince - "Kiss" lyrics, "You don't have to be beautiful to turn me on."

Facebook

Brown University

Jeep

Walmart

Droopy dog

Elvis Presley
Captain Crunch
Sugar Pops
Jerry Lee Lewis – "Great Balls of Fire"
The Little Mermaid
Kentucky Fried Chicken

For Mary Violet and Jonathon, who cheer me on while I follow my path, and who rarely complain about the lack of home cooking.

CHAPTER ONE

Richard

THE KITCHEN DOOR SWUNG OPEN AND ONE OF THE WAITERS emerged carrying a silver tray. The young man's height and breadth gave the impression he'd recently been run through a taffy puller. Richard leaned forward. Bingo! The kid came straight toward them and eased his burden down onto the rack in the center of the table. The greasy aroma of melted cheese, pepperoni, sweet peppers, and onions tickled Richard's enormous nose. He inhaled deeply, savoring the joy of food that was neither the lunch meat sandwiches he had lived on for decades nor the bland, flavorless "health food" served to him at Everest Senior Living Facility. When the kid scooped a slice onto the plate, strings of cheese stretched across open space. Richard forced himself to stifle a whimper.

The first bite burned his mouth. Zesty tomato sauce tingled on his tongue. The crisp golden crust tasted of garlic butter on the bottom and bordered on doughy in the middle.

He knew he'd suffer pain for hours after this, but it was a fair price to pay.

"Oh my gosh," his granddaughter, Burke, mumbled around a mouthful of food. "You weren't kidding. This really is the best pizza in the world."

Richard moaned in reply. He had discovered Huntington, Indiana, by accident decades earlier when passing through. So far as he could tell, that's all people did in Indiana—pass through. He supposed that made the state motto, "The crossroads of America," technically true, if a tad grander than the reality. The town itself could have been any other in a two-hundred-mile radius if not for the Pizza Junction Cafe.

Stanley used the edge of his fork to cut the tip off his slice. He chewed, swallowed, sipped his water. "Mmm. Very nice."

Very nice? Nice? Richard would have screamed the words, but he'd lost control and shoved half a slice in his mouth at once, and he had to focus on not choking to death. By the time he could speak again, Stanley had excused himself and shuffled off to the men's room, leaning heavily on his cane.

For the duration of their acquaintance, Stanley had charged through life, spry as a kid and as annoying as a mosquito in your underpants. A thousand times over, Richard mumbled that the man ought to look and act his age. Now, the sight of the hunched old man shuffling away from them sent a chill down Richard's spine.

Burke chewed her bottom lip and watched him go. Her nails tapped a frantic cadence on the wooden tabletop.

All Richard wanted at that moment was to enjoy his sacred pizza in peace, but Mick Jagger spoke the truth. We don't always get what we want. In fact, in Richard's experience, getting what you wanted was just about a miracle and then, half the time, you ended up sorry you ever asked for it. He drank to clear his throat. "We going to talk about this or what?"

Burke focused on her plate. "I don't even know what to say. It was bad."

Bad didn't begin to cover it. The ghost hunt should have been a milk run. Easy as pie. Simple as sliding off a greasy log backward.

It didn't go that way, though.

It was a complete and utter soup sandwich.

Burke had been the one to stumble across the story in the newspaper. Three teenagers died inside an abandoned home in the suburbs of Chicago. Local legend claimed that a member of the house's building crew died during the building's construction. It had been haunted ever since. A long string of owners experienced strange and frightening sights and sounds. A child died in the night. The coroner said crib death, but the neighbors talked about flickering lights and mysterious shadows darting across the windows. Over time, it became impossible to sell the place. For the past several years, the house sat vacant, a haven for homeless people and youngsters up to no good.

The kids who died went there on a dare. Who was brave enough to spend the night in the haunted house?

They'd been brave.

Now they were dead.

Richard, Stanley, and Burke agreed to the same simple plan they'd used on a dozen other ghost hunts. Go in. Wait for the thing to show itself. Stanley would bind the wayward spirit in iron while Richard and Burke performed a banishment spell. A flash of light and a gust of hot, sulfur-scented wind, and the ghost would move on to wherever such things went.

Sure, they all knew that something could go sideways, but

Richard never thought that the something would be Stanley. He believed in Stanley. He counted on him. Stanley had saved Richard's life over and again. He taught Richard how to be a hunter. Even The Devil Herself held a healthy respect for Stanley. And, yeah, maybe he'd been a little off his game lately, but whoever would have guessed that Stan freakin' Kapcheck would lose his guts over a ghost?

Maybe Burke guessed. At the last minute, she'd offered to trade jobs with Stanley. The binding required lifting and throwing the heavy chains. The person doing that faced a significantly higher chance of being knocked across the room by the ghost. Go figure, but being banished for eternity tended to raise the ire of restless spirits.

"Your bad leg's been bothering you. You should read the spell this time," she'd said.

Stanley refused. "No one reads the Latin more precisely than you. I'll do the grunt work. You work your magic."

In an empty room coated in dust and cobwebs, they'd sat on old milk crates and waited. The brass bowl and the ingredients for the spell lay spread out on the floor in front of Richard. Burke held the spell book on her lap. The chains coiled at Stanley's feet glimmered like serpents in the dim light of the battery-operated lantern.

Shortly after midnight, the room grew cold enough for them to see their breath and the lantern began to flicker. Richard reached for the bundle of white sage and a book of matches. Stanley stood and lifted a portion of the chain.

Oily gray smoke hissed through the vent and formed into a shape vaguely reminiscent of a young man. He regarded the three hunters with eyes of flickering red and then shrieked. Monsters always shrieked. Richard found it annoying. He lit the sage on fire and dropped it in the bowl. An earthy aroma drifted upward with the curling white smoke.

Burke began reciting the Latin text, but Stanley stood frozen and wide eyed. His hands trembled, raising a metallic jingling from the chains. The ghost shot toward Stanley and he jerked back, stumbled over a milk crate, hit the floor, curled into a ball, and started crying like a baby.

Richard stopped mixing the ingredients in the bowl and stared with his mouth hanging open. He'd once watched Stanley hold his ground against a dozen monsters. The cocky SOB had actually laughed while fighting them. Now he fell to pieces like a little girl at the sight of a single ghost?

Burke's voice took on a sharp note of intensity and the spirit's attention shifted to the two of them.

Richard reached for a bag of goofer dust, but an invisible force slammed into his chest and knocked him off his stool.

Burke lunged for the iron chains. From the corner of his eye, Richard saw a fireball fly toward her and catch the back of her shirt. She rolled across the floor to squelch the flames and the ghost shot toward her.

Richard scrambled on hands and knees toward the chains, but she shouted at him, "You're almost done! Forget the chain, finish the spell!"

The brass bowl had tipped onto its side. He hoped the meager contents that remained unspilled would be enough to accomplish their goal. He added a splash of holy water and cut his finger to squeeze out three drops of blood.

Icy cold hands wrapped around his throat. Tears sprang to his eyes, blurring the world around him. His existence dwindled down to Burke's frantic voice.

"Per istam sanctam unctionem et suam piissimam misericordiam

adiuvet te deminus gratia spiritus sancti, ut a peccatis liberatum te salvet atque propitious alleviet!"

The spirit shrieked and burst into a cloud of dust that reeked of rotten eggs.

Richard choked and coughed like a John Deere tractor running on moonshine. Ragged breath whistled through his bruised windpipe.

Stanley sobbed.

The three of them staggered outside. They sought the familiar comfort of their 1959 Cadillac convertible. None of them spoke about Stanley's failure. What was there to say? The most feared hunter of supernatural creatures in the world had lost his nerve.

They found a rest stop and cleaned themselves up. Burke took a pair of scissors to her scraggly mess of singed curls and cut her hair so short you'd have thought she was a new recruit on her first day of basic training. Together, they retreated from the big city and headed east. Stanley slept in the backseat while Burke followed Richard's directions to the little green and gray restaurant next to the railroad tracks.

OUTSIDE PIZZA JUNCTION, EVERY HALF HOUR OR SO, A ROW of diesel engines hauled a rumbling behemoth past the building at frightening speeds. The ground quaked and the odor of spent fuel lingered in the train's wake. The café, a former train depot, sat as close to the edge of the tracks as possible, and diners pointed out the windows or raced onto the deck to watch when the trains roared by. The intimate encounter with enormous power left a person feeling dizzy and small.

Servers waited for the horns and clanging traffic signals to settle before carrying on, collecting orders for soft drinks, submarine sandwiches, and pizza.

Cool air seeped through the multi-pane windows while the heater blew hot breath down from above. While Stanley had shared the corner booth with them, nursing his cup of tea, Burke had spoken with undue animation. A huge smile showed off her straight white teeth and the freckles dotting her brown cheeks. The second he'd excused himself to use the restroom, she dropped the cheerful façade.

"It was bad," Richard agreed with her assessment of their hunt.

"I'm so worried about him."

Richard reached for a second slice of pizza and agreed again. "It ain't natural to be staggering along like he is. Or... well...it is natural. And that ain't natural for Stanley."

"We have to do something."

"What are we going to do?"

"Maybe we need to find another case. Something easier. He needs to keep his mind occupied." She sighed and ran a hand across her short hair. "He needs a win."

Richard leveled a gaze at her. "He ain't in no shape to be hunting. Ain't no hunt easier than a ghost hunt and he fell apart. Something's broke in him."

Burke threw her hands up and let them slap down onto the table. Silverware clanked and rattled against the plates. "Can you blame him?"

Two old women in the next booth scowled in their direction.

Richard scowled back at them.

They huffed before resuming their hushed conversation.

Burke leaned in and lowered her voice, "We've known

Stanley less than a year. In that time, he's broken his leg, been captured and tortured by The Devil, nearly died from heat stroke, been stabbed in the heart, and had the dark half of his soul ripped off and reattached. He's almost a hundred and fifty years old. How much can a man take?"

Richard finished chewing and debated if he had room for a third slice. He burped and cleared some space. "What's your point?"

"He's had a rough few months, don't you think?"

"Ain't we all?"

Burke ate in thoughtful silence.

Stanley returned to the table and finished his single slice.

Richard smacked his gums and made a mental note to stock up on prune juice on the way to the hotel. All this cheese was bound to glue his innards together.

Burke dropped her fork onto her plate and stalked off toward the ladies' room.

Richard looked at Stanley. "Guess she had to go."

Stanley inclined his head. "Indeed." He sipped his tea.

Maybe it would be the right thing to bring up the subject and air it out. Maybe he should ask what happened. Maybe the old boy just needed some time, or a drink stiffer than tea, or the love of a good woman. Who the heck knew?

Maybe it would be best to talk, but it was much easier and more pleasant to stay quiet and enjoy the food.

CHAPTER TWO

Burke

BURKE LOCKED THE BATHROOM DOOR AND PRESSED HER shoulder blades against it, letting her head fall back against the painted wood. Safely tucked away from the world, she let her tears come. They spilled over the dams of her lids, and wove silvery tracks along her cheekbones, and dripped from her face. She didn't sob or scream. She was not a woman inclined toward hysterics, but she needed to weep.

Memories came of meeting Stanley for the first time in a hospital when he'd broken his leg. She'd schemed with him when he allowed The Devil to kidnap him for the sake of the greater good. She'd held his lifeless body in her arms when he was stabbed. For all that, when she thought of Stanley, she didn't picture him hurt or in distress. She thought of him as constantly defying danger and laughing at death.

But he wasn't like that any longer. He'd become a timid old man, frightened of his own shadow.

She brushed the tears away with her fingertips and pushed

away from the door. The water from the faucet smelled strongly of chlorine, but it ran cool as a mountain stream. She splashed some on her face and dried off with the scratchy brown paper towels from the dispenser.

"All right, pull yourself together," she told the woman in the mirror. "There is a solution to every problem. What action can you take?"

The woman in the mirror stared back at her with wide brown eyes full of accusation. *You let Stanley give himself over to The Devil. You did nothing to save him from that knife. Time and again, you allowed him to take the hard blows for the team, but none of that compares to the colossal price he paid to save you from The Daughters of Kali. Whatever is wrong with him now is on you. For a century, Stanley Kapcheck hunted and thrived. One year with you and he's done in.*

Her grandfather spoke the truth.

Something in Stanley was broken and it was broken because of her stupid mistakes.

"I broke it. I'll fix it," she told her reflection. But that was a fool's errand and she knew it. One person can't fix another person's broken spirit. That kind of healing comes from within or it never comes.

The Eagles' song, *Witchy Woman*, broke through her thoughts. She pulled her phone from her pocket, glanced at the screen, and flicked the touchscreen to answer the call.

"Hey, Mom."

"Guess where I am?" Maddie's breathless joy brought a smile to Burke's lips.

Burke turned and leaned one hip against the counter. She couldn't resist teasing just a little. "At home watching talk shows?"

"As if I ever did that. You know me better than that."

Burke grinned. Her mother was always the picture of the prim and proper lady. "Are you still in bed, lounging next to your handsome lover?"

"Burke Dakota! Why would you say such a thing?"

She feigned innocence, "What? Luke is handsome, don't you think?"

Her mother sputtered. "Luke and I are very good friends. We enjoy one another's company. That's all."

"Mom, the man took you on a cruise and he buys you red roses every Saturday. He's more than a friend." In fact, Luke Castleberry was so completely, obviously head-over-heels in love with Maddie that Burke was a little surprised the man hadn't proposed yet.

"Fine. He's a...what do they call it now? A friend with benefits."

If Burke had taken a drink, she would have spit it out.

"Why are you laughing at me?" her mother asked.

It felt fantastic to have something to laugh at. "You probably shouldn't use that term, Mom. I don't think it means what you think it means."

Maddie sighed.

Burke imagined she could hear her mother's eyes rolling.

"Do you want to know where I am or not?" Maddie snapped.

Burke considered pushing a little further but decided it would be wise to let the matter drop before teasing turned into a real argument. "The curiosity is killing me. Where are you?"

"In the Bahamas!"

Whatever Burke had been expecting, it wasn't that. "How in the world did you end up in the Bahamas?"

Maddie laughed. She sounded freer and more genuinely

happy than she had in a very long time. "My friend surprised me with another cruise. I think he's trying to make me fat. I swear, you get on these ships and they start feeding you, and the eating never stops. You shop and gamble and watch these wild stage shows, and all the while you're eating. Then you go ashore and vendors are selling you food. The second you get back to the boat, they feed you again."

"Wow! Mom, I don't know what to say. It sounds wonderful."

Maddie's voice rasped across the fine-grain sandpaper of emotion. "It is wonderful, Burke. After your father... I... He..."

"I know, Mom. I know how much you loved him and how hard it was, but he would have wanted this for you. He would have wanted you to keep living and be happy, to heal and move on." Tears rolled down her cheeks again. Was it possible to get dehydrated from being overly emotional?

"Thank you for saying that, for understanding. That's exactly how I feel. The scars are still there. I'll always miss him, but there's something about being out here in the open ocean that heals the soul."

The words clanged loud as church bells in Burke's mind.

Healing.

That was precisely what Stanley needed. He didn't need more drama, more fear, more adrenaline. He needed time and space to heal. Maybe a week in the sun would do it—a real vacation. That could be the key to bringing Stanley back to them. Really, what was the worst that could happen? A sunburn? Indigestion from all the rich food?

She realized her mother waited for a response and mumbled something about everything sounding great. They said their goodbyes and shared their love and Burke pressed the red button to hang up, marveling that she'd had an entire conversation with her mother without getting angry. Miracles could happen.

BURKE CLEANED THE STREAKS OF MASCARA FROM HER FACE and exited the ladies' room. She stopped at the end of the little hallway and peered out. Her grandfather and Stanley sat in silence. Grandpa munched on what must be his fourth slice of pizza by now. He'd be in misery later and insist the food was worth it. With Stanley's back to her, she couldn't possibly discern Stanley's expression, but he sat unmoving, his head tilted toward the window.

She squared her shoulders. *I can fix this.*

Long strides carried her across the small space in seconds, and she slipped onto the seat next to her grandfather.

She took in the dark circles under Stanley's eyes and the unhealthy pallor of his ghostly white skin. Her resolve redoubled. "We should go on vacation."

Both men stared at her.

She grinned. "I'm serious. We drive around and chase these hunting jobs but staying in hotels is hardly the same as a real vacation."

Stanley blinked like a baby owl.

Richard turned sideways in his seat and regarded her as if she suggested that they cut off their arms for entertainment.

"Mom called. Do you know where she is?"

"Shacked up with Castleberry?" Richard guessed.

Burke snorted. "Well, yeah, sort of, though she denies it and puts all sorts of other names to it. Anyway, she's on a cruise ship in the Bahamas."

"She just got off a cruise ship in Antarctica. Why're they on another one?"

"The Mediterranean," Burke corrected. "And I imagine they're on another because it's that much fun. She went on and on about the food. Imagine—a week of sunshine and fine dining in the middle of this endless gray winter. It's exactly what we need."

Stanley shrugged his thin shoulders. "I don't know. It sounds..." His gaze wandered toward the window where a train rumbled by, rattling the joints of building and diners alike.

Richard watched the other man for a long moment. His gaze traveled downward, and Burke saw what must have caught his attention. Stanley, always dapper and perfectly groomed, had a spot of tomato sauce on his shirt. The sight of it caused Burke's eyes to burn. She blinked the tears away and forced the most cheerful tone she could muster, "Well? What do you think? I can book it on my phone, and we could be boarding the boat the day after tomorrow."

Richard ran one hand through his wispy white hair. "A cruise, huh? Sounds good. Great. Sunshine and warmth for these old bones? Pretty girls with them drinks that have the little umbrellas in them. Let's do it."

Stanley's bony chest rose and fell with a long sigh. "Whatever you all think is best."

She expressed her fake excitement and poked at the pizza on her plate, but her appetite had deserted her. If this didn't work... No. It would work. It had to.

CHAPTER THREE

Gordon

GORDON STOOD IN THE MORGUE, WATCHING THE DOCTOR and his assistant stock the shelves and cabinets and take inventory. He told himself it was the cool air that caused the goosebumps on his arms, but he knew there was more to it. Those supplies should not have to be replaced. Not so soon. Not so often. True, cruises attracted an older clientele and death at sea was far from unusual, but so many deaths, and all the same way...

Frustrated by his impotence, he turned on his heel and set off on a check of other areas. Even at this ungodly hour, with the great blazing circle of the sun only starting to peek above the eastern horizon, the ship buzzed with activity. One week ago, 3,127 passengers boarded the *Diversion* for the vacation getaway of a lifetime. One day ago, 3,123 disembarked on their own. The other four were carried off in body bags and handed over to weeping relatives who said again and again that they couldn't understand it. He'd been in such good health. He just had a checkup. How? Why?

Gordon oversaw the removal of the bodies. Just like he'd overseen the process the week before, and the week before that.

In a few short hours, 3,134 new passengers would board.

He wondered how many of them would sail if they understood that, on this ship, it was almost guaranteed they all wouldn't return home alive.

He rubbed his eyes. The result didn't have to be the same. He could solve this. He could figure this out. He had to. If not, why else was he here?

Ike, the activities director, bustled around the corner, his hips twitching back and forth like a twenty-year-old girl on a Paris runway. Gordon struggled to fit the pieces of Ike's personality together. He'd never met a man bigger, stronger or more athletic than Ike. He resembled a pro-wrestler, but he walked and acted like a flighty young woman. He had no fear of the sea in any condition, but he'd once screamed and fled the room at the sight of a little gray mouse. Twelve years traveling the world with the military had taught Gordon not to judge. People were people and the only weird ones were those who claimed to be normal, but in his experience, most effeminate men were more like the fruity little lounge singer who fancied himself Prince's twin soul. And go figure, the lounge singer favored girls.

Ike beamed at him. "Good morning, Mr. Westchester."

Gordon nodded in return. "Ike."

"Ready for another fantastic week?"

No one else was around.

Ike was an unusual guy, but Gordon had the distinct feeling

he knew more than the average crew member about the things that happened aboard ship; plus, he had a mind like a steel trap. Tell him anything and he'd remember for life. "Can I ask you something?"

Ike hugged his clipboard to his massive chest. "Well, sure. I'm always happy to help."

"Are you worried?"

"About what? We've got nothing but blue skies in the forecast. The ship's sound as any seagoing vessel."

"People die on this ship," Gordon said.

Ike's smile faded. "The doctor says it's natural."

"Not exactly. The doctor says he can't find any evidence of foul play."

"It's just a string of bad luck. It'll pass. It probably already has. You'll see. This week will be great."

Gordon prayed the big guy was right. "Have you seen anything strange? Anything at all?"

"Sweetheart, you could film the world's best reality show based on what I've seen on this ship."

Gordon glared at him. "You know what I mean."

Ike nodded. "I'll tell you this. Everybody's sleeping with anybody. Somebody's got an onshore connection for reefer and they're running a happy little side-business. That old dame living on the high roller deck has a bottle tan, and the Captain's new cufflinks cost more than a man in his pay range should be spending, but they really are fabulous."

Gordon ground his teeth together. "Forget it." He tried to step past, but Ike put a gentle hand on his arm.

"You're good at your job, Gordon. If I see anything that I think you should know, I promise I'll tell you."

"Do you think the deaths are natural?" Gordon asked him.

Ike took a deep breath. "I hope so."

Gordon finished his rounds, touched base with his staff, and found a shady corner in the main lobby. From there, he had a clear view of the boarding passengers as they walked, rolled, and hobbled up the gangplank, and came blinking into the grand lobby to shake hands with their charming captain.

Northrup was in fine form. Not a wrinkle marred his fabulous white uniform. Not a silver hair dared rebel against perfect alignment. They could jettison the fuel and power the ship with that brilliant smile.

Gordon's gut tightened. His entire adult life had been spent fighting for the safety and freedom of others, and instinct honed over decades told him that the real man behind the captain's idiotic grin was cunning and self-serving and up to no good.

ON THE FIRST NIGHT OF EVERY CRUISE, DINERS CLOGGED THE entrance to the dining room, gaping as though they'd never seen linen tablecloths or servers in waistcoats before. They wandered to their tables like chubby sheep behind the hosts and talked too loudly when introducing themselves to their tablemates. Half of them were already drunk and would stay that way for the duration of the journey.

Gordon hated the dining room. Of all the rooms aboard ship, it was his least favorite. Worse even than the morgue. At least the morgue was quiet. A man could think in there. Nevertheless, following the food was pretty much a sure way to find the captain.

Sure enough, he already sat at his table with a handful of

VIP guests. The Captain saw Gordon coming and his ever-present smile wilted at the edges. By the time Gordon arrived at the table, Captain Northrup had recovered enough to act happy to see him.

"Mr. Westchester! Have you come to join us? Please meet my guests, Mr. and Mrs. Knapp, Dr. Keller, and Reverend and Mrs. Price."

Gordon gave a half-hearted nod of acknowledgment to the group and tried not to stare at the extraordinary mole on Mrs. Price's chin. "May I have a word?" he asked the captain.

"We were just about to order drinks. Could you wait, perhaps, until tomorrow?"

"I'm afraid not."

The captain's smile widened, giving him the appearance of a grinning maniac. "Well, then, excuse me, folks. Duty calls."

Gordon led him to a relatively quiet nearby corner. The distance plus the din of the dining room offered enough cover to allow them to speak with some level of privacy. "Did you look over the files I gave you?"

Captain Northrup lifted one shoulder. "It's been a busy few days. I'll get to them."

"Every day is busy, Captain. I thought I emphasized the critical nature of my request."

"Gordon, Gordon"—he shook his head—"every request you make is critical, but not everything can be a crisis. We must deal with each moment as it comes."

Gordon swallowed words he dearly wanted to say and forced a more polite response, "The request is critical because, if we don't take some kind of action, the moment we will be dealing with is the moment someone is reported dead. Again. Is that what you want?"

"Old people die, Gordon. It's a sad, unavoidable truth."

"Nobody dies for no reason, not even old people, certainly not large numbers of perfectly healthy old people."

The captain puffed his cheeks out like a blowfish. "I don't know that I'd call three or four a large number."

"Three or four a week," Gordon reminded him. "Once, there were five. How much longer do you think they're going to keep this ship running under your command if this continues?"

His eyes narrowed. "What are you saying?"

"I'm saying the same thing I've been saying for months. We need to figure out what's going on and I can't do that alone. Now, did you request the background checks I asked for on the new hires?"

"I'll get to it."

Gordon gritted his teeth. "I'd suggest sooner rather than later."

"I don't see the rush. I mean, if anything untoward is happening aboard this ship, and I'm quite certain it is not, the new hires can't have had anything to do with it. They're new, after all."

"So, you see no reason to properly vet them?"

"They all had references that checked out or they wouldn't have been hired in the first place. Have some faith in the HR people back home, Gordo. Everything will be fine. Mark my words." He slapped him on the back. "Take the night off, my friend. Have a drink on the deck and soak in the scenery. We're in one of the most beautiful parts of the globe."

The muscles in Gordon's arm twitched. Had he ever wanted to hit anyone so badly? Probably, but at the moment, he couldn't think who. Before he did anything he regretted, he marched past the captain and pushed his way through the crowd at the door. He'd go to his office and review his notes again. Maybe this time something would pop out at him and he'd figure out what the hell was going on. Nine-hundredth time was a charm.

CHAPTER FOUR

Richard

IN THE PREDAWN HOURS, THE GAS STATION GLOWED LIKE A space station beside the highway. A tropical breeze carried the scent of the ocean through the darkness. Richard took a deep breath. The fresh air smelled significantly better than the men's room. When would the folks designing air fresheners realize that adding perfume to sewage was not an improvement?

He crossed the tarmac through a thin cloud of insects and found Burke sitting on the Caddy's trunk, waiting for the gas pump to click off automatically. The classic car stood out on the highway—a work of art amidst a clutter of look-alike economy cars. It drove like a dream and carried them in comfort. He could list a hundred things he loved about that car, but the one major downside was that keeping the gas tank full was akin to pouring fuel into a bottomless pit.

"Where's Stan?" he asked.

Burke made a vague gesture toward the building. "Said he needed to buy a few things. You okay?"

"Fine as frog's hair. Why wouldn't I be?"

Her ultra-short hair made it much more obvious when she arched a brow at him. "You've made a lot of trips to the men's room since Huntington."

The truth was that, as predicted, his guts had been tied in knots since the night after the heavenly pizza. It seemed the worst was over though, and he was hopeful about being able to enjoy the much-talked-about cruise ship food later that day. At any rate, he harbored no desire at all to discuss his bowels with his granddaughter. "Well, I'm fine," he told her.

She twisted her mouth into a skeptical expression, but at least she let the subject drop.

Richard peeked in the direction of the store. No sign of Stanley yet. He drew closer to Burke. "Listen, kid. I been thinkin'. What if this ain't the best thing for Stan?"

She raised her chin a fraction of an inch—a warning to proceed with caution. "I thought we were agreed."

Richard snatched the squeegee out of the tub attached to the garbage can next to the gas pump and started smearing blue-tinted water across the bug-splattered windshield.

The gas pump clicked off and Burke hopped down to replace the nozzle and screw on the cap. She leaned one hip against the side of the car and regarded him with laser eyes. "You're not backing out now that we're all the way down here, are you?"

He kept his eyes on his task. "No. I ain't backing out."

"Because you agreed this would be good for Stanley. He needs rest. He needs time to heal."

Richard dragged the rubber edge of the squeegee across the

glass. The resulting squeak echoed off the aluminum ceiling over the fueling area. In the distance, the engines of several tractor-trailers rumbled. He glanced over at the front doors of the store. Still no sign of Stanley. "Maybe," he conceded.

"Maybe? Grandpa, rest is—"

"Rest is what almost killed me," he blurted. The frustration behind his outburst cooled as fast as it flared. He finished cleaning the windshield and walked around the car to drop the squeegee back into the bucket. Looking directly into the girl's eyes made it too hard to speak, so he studied the advertisements on the side of the gas pump. "Your mother sent me to Everest to rest and to heal. That's what she said. But every old fart in that place knew full good and well that they'd been sent there to die. So that's what they did. They died inside. Then they sat around in front of the fancy flat-screen televisions waiting for their shriveled up old bodies to figure out that they were supposed to follow suit. What if giving Stanley a chance to rest causes him to give up and die?"

Burke came close and leaned against the car next to him. "Going on a cruise isn't the same as moving into a nursing home, Grandpa. I'm sorry you felt that way, but it's apples and oranges. A cruise is more like a super-safe, very-well-planned adventure. I mean, did you look at the stops? When we get to Puerto Rico, there's an old ruin there with dungeons and everything. Hiking around a place like that isn't anything like sitting indoors and watching The Weather Channel."

He shrugged one shoulder. "The Weather Channel ain't all bad."

"Maybe this is the wrong thing to do. Maybe it'll be the greatest week of our lives. We can't know for sure how things will work out, but we need to stick to the plan. It's all we have right now." She took his hand. "Think of it this way. Stanley says that hunters are always led to their hunts, right? They kind of pop up in your path, right?"

"Yeah. That's what he says."

"And it's always been true for us. Think about it. Hunts just kind of fall into our laps. Even when we went to Mom's for a visit, right?"

He glanced at her from the side of his eye. "I suppose so," he agreed.

"But we haven't come across so much as a rumor of anything hinky since we left Chicago. Maybe that means the universe wants us to go on this vacation. Maybe it's God's way of showing us He's giving his blessing to our few days in the sun."

Richard squeezed her hand. "Yeah. Maybe." But a little voice deep down inside shouted for his attention. Burke's words stirred an idea. It took a minute to latch onto it, but once he did, it caused him to stand straighter. He squinted and made out Stanley, standing at the cash register. He only had a minute before the old peacock rejoined them. "What if we're being led?"

Burke tilted her head. "Isn't that what I just said?"

"No. You said we were being allowed to take a rest. What if this isn't a rest? What if there's a hunt on that ship?"

"Grandpa—"

"No, hear me out."

Stanley passed some cash over the counter. The elderly redhead running the register smiled.

"You hear about weird things happening out at sea all the time, right? No reason that boat can't hold a ghost."

She opened her mouth to speak again, but he rushed on to stop her, "Or maybe it ain't the boat. You said there's a tour of dungeons. You think there's a dungeon in the world that don't hold at least one vengeful spirit or bloodthirsty monster? Heck. Maybe there's a sea monster causing trouble. Being in the ocean opens up a whole new world of possibility." He couldn't determine if fear or excitement caused the pounding in his heart. He'd learned that the line separating the two could be thinner than the last hair on old-bald-Stanley's head.

"Grandpa, seriously, it is not a good idea to—"

The door of the store swung open and Stanley emerged carrying a plastic bag.

Burke spun around so Stanley couldn't read her lips. "Do *not* start talking to him about hunting on the ship," she whispered.

Richard fiddled with his hearing aid. "Speak up. Can't hear you."

"Grandpa," she hissed.

He grinned at her, looked over her shoulder toward Stanley, and asked, "Everything okay in there? Almost turned another year older waiting on you."

Stanley held up the bag. "I waited for a fresh batch of sausage sandwiches. I thought they'd be better than the ones that have been under the heat lamp."

"In that case, the delay is forgiven," Richard said. The idea of a hot sausage sandwich made his mouth water—a good sign that his body had recovered from the pizza.

Stanley studied the scene. "Everything all right out here?"

Burke turned and plastered a big fake smile across her face. "Fine. Yes. Great. Ready to go? We better hit the road if we want to make it to Miami before boarding time."

Stanley hesitated, then nodded without saying more. He climbed into the back seat.

"Don't you dare bring up ghost hunts and sea monsters,"

Burke said out of the corner of her mouth as she walked around to the driver's door.

Richard slipped into the car without saying anything, but he wasn't about to let the idea go. Stanley always used to drive. If he'd turned into a backseat passenger, then a good sea monster kill could be the greatest thing in the world for him. The ghost hunt was probably just a one-off. Everybody had bad days. Stanley needed to get back on the horse and Richard was determined not to miss an opportunity for him to do it.

By mid-morning, the three hunters stood on the broad, paved walkway and stared at the ship. Bright stripes and abstract patterns adorned the sides of the gleaming white behemoth. The sun, slightly behind them at that hour, glimmered from little iridescent details in the paint, giving the impression that the Brobdingnagian craft had sprouted straight from the sparkling sea upon which Gulliver had traveled.

"That's a big boat," Richard said.

Burke nodded. "Yup. You could live in there. There are restaurants and stores, spas, doctors' offices, a bowling alley, a casino, a waterslide—"

"I ain't going on no waterslide," Richard interrupted.

"But you could, if you were so inclined," Burke said.

"I ain't inclined." He hoisted his duffle a little higher on his shoulder.

She let the subject drop and led them toward the ramp, where a row of impossibly beautiful people in neatly pressed uniforms waited to greet them with the well-practiced smiles of experienced hospitality workers.

Stanley shuffled along in front of Richard. He returned the greetings with his standard excessive politeness but no real interest.

They traversed up the rattling metal gangplank, crossing above the ripples that lapped against the hull of the ship. Richard noticed a dead fish drifting along in the current, belly up, and deliberately chose not to take it as an omen. Stepping from the bright sun into the shade of the ship's interior left him temporarily blinded. As his eyes adjusted, a massive lobby materialized in front of him. Thick navy-blue carpet stretched across a wide expanse dominated by a sweeping central staircase. Crystal and gilt chandeliers glittered overhead. A glass elevator slid up one wall, carrying occupants toward a stained-glass mosaic of a tropical scene.

A man in head-to-toe white with a black silk necktie and golden epaulets greeted them. He was about the same size and weight as Richard, but the similarities ended there. He had a deep tan with distinct white sunglass shapes around his eyes and a full head of salt and pepper hair that lay in tidy waves against his scalp. "Welcome aboard the *Diversion*. I'm Captain Roy Northrup."

Burke extended her hand and they shook. "We're very excited. We've never been on a cruise before."

Well, the second half of that statement's true, Richard thought. He scanned the crowd of chubby old folks in short pants with skepticism.

The captain leaned forward as if imparting a secret. "You're going to love it. Allow me to introduce our Activities Director, Ike Terry. Mr. Terry has the most extraordinary week planned for us! He's a master at what he does. I tell you, our guests just can't stop smiling, even after they leave here."

Richard's gaze shifted from the captain's face and smacked

into the chest of a mountain of a man. A little more than half a foot up from the chest, he found a face that reminded him of no one so much as Mr. Clean. Apart from the man's golden-brown complexion, the resemblance was uncanny. When the guy reached to shake hands, the seams of his navy and white uniform strained and stretched over the hulking muscles of his shoulders and arms. Richard could swear he felt the ship tilt slightly under his weight.

"Welcome aboard, Miss..."

"Martin," Burke said, shaking his hand. "Please, call me Burke." She stepped away so Richard and Stanley could step forward. "This is my grandfather, Richard, and our dear friend, Stanley."

Richard let the man's gargantuan paw crush his hand for a brief moment.

"A pleasure to make your acquaintance," Stanley said when his turn came around.

Gigantor's eyes settled on Stanley and, for the first time in weeks, Richard saw the spark of interest so many strangers expressed upon first meeting Stanley. "The pleasure is all mine, Stanley."

Richard rolled his eyes.

"Well, we shouldn't take any more of your time. We're holding up the line," Burke said.

"I'm sure I'll be seeing you again," Ike replied without looking away from Stan.

Richard harrumphed and hoisted his bag up again. Be nice to get somewhere he could set the blasted thing down.

Burke checked the papers in her hand and the signs posted about the lobby before leading them around the side of the staircase.

Maybe everyone left smiling, but just then, most of the

people he saw wore dazed, disoriented expressions that matched his own state of mind. The bulk of the passengers appeared to be as old as him and as infirm as Stanley, and he wondered about the economic wisdom of installing a water-slide on a ship used by this particular crowd. Then, he noticed a woman in a long red sundress. She was the kind of woman who was clearly used to being noticed. She leaned against the wall, sipping from a martini glass and watching the crowd. Diamonds and rubies dripped from her ears, throat, fingers, and wrists. The lines around her sapphire eyes placed her close to his own age, but the sparkle in her grin added to the youthful, mischievous aura that emanated from her. She raised her glass in his direction.

"Grandpa? You coming?" Burke asked over her shoulder.

He'd fallen behind Burke and Stanley and hurried to catch up. When he peeked back as they rounded the corner, she was watching him. A hot blush rose up from his collar and he ducked around the bend, grateful to escape her line of sight.

The elevator carried them four levels up. Burke had reserved three adjacent rooms and she passed out the keys. "Don't forget, we have to be on deck in thirty-five minutes for the safety spiel," she reminded them.

Stanley accepted his key from her with a quiet thank you and disappeared into his room.

Richard entered his own space—an area marginally bigger than the average walk-in closet, but lushly appointed, and with a large window that would offer a view of water and more water once they got underway. He tossed the duffle in the itty-bitty closet and dropped onto the bed with the remote control, happy to be off his feet and well away from the gauntlet of grinning greeters.

He wondered idly if anyone would notice if he didn't show

up for the safety lecture. Did they do a roll call or something? He imagined how embarrassing it would be to have four thousand passengers standing around waiting for him to arrive and resolved not to be late. *I'm doing this for Stanley*, he reminded himself.

His stomach rumbled. After the thing on deck, they'd be off to sea. Dinner would be served. All anyone talked about when it came to these cruises was the food. The dining experience was definitely something to look forward to.

It turned out that the most interesting part of the lecture was the tall, slim woman with skin like black silk and a French accent. The rest was nonsense about lifeboats and floatation devices. Richard kept himself alert for the duration of her spiel by studying the folks around him, looking for anything that might lead them to a hunt. There appeared to be as many wrinkles and fat rolls as there were waves in the ocean, but not a fang or a red glowing eye among the bunch. Not that that necessarily meant anything. Monsters walked undetected among humans all the time.

When the woman finished her talk, the larger part of the crowd made their way to the railing. They cheered and called out to the folks watching and waving from the dock below. The ship's horn blew, sending vibrations through the floor beneath their feet. Gulls circled overhead, screaming at one another. Streamers were blasted out over the crowd and, so slowly it was almost imperceptible, the ship began to move. Gradually, Miami faded into the distance.

"I can't believe it took me over forty years to go on a sea voyage," Burke said. "Honestly, such a thing never even occurred to me before Mom and Luke did it. I mean, I knew about cruises, I just never considered going on one."

Richard felt the spirit of his sweet Barbara draw near.

Perhaps, if they'd had more time, she would have talked him into this nonsense. It seemed like something she would have loved—travel, people, sunshine, dancing. No doubt, Barbara would have enjoyed both the waterslide and the ridiculous ice bar.

Stanley took a deep breath of the warm sea air. "I celebrated my twentieth birthday aboard a ship as opulent as any royal sailing vessel. It took us ten days to get to Ellis Island. I spent all ten drunk and in the arms of women. Busar had to bribe the immigration officials to let me in. I could barely remain conscious long enough to answer their questions."

Richard slapped him on the back. "Sowing youth's wild oats, eh?"

"Mourning the death of my mother," Stanley replied.

Burke's shoulders slumped. "Oh, Lord. I dragged you onto this ship to help you feel better and all the while... Why didn't you say anything?"

He rested his hand over hers. "I thought it was a good idea. I promise to be somewhat more temperate than I was back then."

They trooped back down to their rooms and changed into dinner clothes. Richard had agreed, with what he felt was good grace, to a button-front shirt and a sports jacket, but he drew the line at wearing a tie.

Burke reminded him of an Egyptian goddess in her thin white cotton dress with a wide collar of golden beads.

Stanley emerged from his room in a three-piece suit, complete with bowtie and pocket square. Leaning on his cane with its fancy silver handle, he looked very much the part of a British dandy. True, his shoes lacked their usual shine and a few wrinkles marred the smooth lines of his formerly well-tailored suit, but all things considered, he looked sharp.

Richard considered telling him so and then rejected the idea. No need to go overboard.

Back upstairs, they followed the herd of humanity to the Grand Dining Salon. Ike, the activities director, greeted them at the door. "Burke, you're a vision."

"Thank you, Mr. Terry."

"Ike, please," he said before turning to Richard. "Richard, I hope you enjoy your dinner."

Richard shook hands, impressed by the giant's memory. He started to mention it, but Ike already held Stanley's hand between his bear paws.

"I say, Stanley, you do have a fabulous flair for fashion." His gaze ranged down the full length of Stanley's body and back up again.

"Aren't you kind to say so," Stanley replied.

A gruff-looking guy with a scowl that made Richard feel positively cheerful by comparison, shouldered his way past Ike.

Ike's gaze followed him for a split-second before flicking in the direction from which he'd come. The ship's captain was hurrying off in the opposite direction. Ike dropped Stanley's hand.

"Grandpa?" Burke and a pretty young hostess in a classy black dress stood waiting for them.

"Well, go on, then. I'm coming," Richard told them.

Earlier, Burke had explained that, just like at summer camp, they'd be eating with pre-assigned tablemates.

"Here we are, table thirteen. Your server for the week will be Luca. Enjoy your dinner."

The martini glass lady from the lobby sat at the table, grinning up at him. She'd exchanged her rubies for purple jewels. The purple silk of her dress flowed over her feminine curves.

"This is gonna be fun," she said without shifting her eyes from Richard.

Richard shuffled around the table to put Burke and Stanley between the woman and himself and then realized with a sinking sensation he now sat directly in her line of sight.

A young couple, who appeared physically incapable of being more than three inches away from each other for even a few seconds, joined them. Not long after that, the hostess seated an elderly couple who didn't seem to be speaking to one another. Then Luca materialized out of nowhere.

The waiter stood six feet tall, every angle sharp—the ridge on his nose, the cut of his jaw, even the perfect creases on his slacks and the sleeves of his heavily starched, bright-white shirt. Bumping into the guy could result in a severed limb. When he spoke, even his words sliced across the air as clear and honed as a scalpel. Each syllable possessed its own carefully crafted space. "Good evening and welcome to the *Diversion*'s Grand Dining Salon. My name is Luca, and I will be serving you for the duration of this fantastic voyage. I was born and raised in Macedonia, and I have always dreamed of traveling the world." He held out arms as long as broomsticks. "I am living proof that dreams really do come true, yes? Now it is my honor to share this wondrous experience with you good people. I am very excited." He bounced on his toes and clapped his hands together. The boy was either genuinely excited or an actor deserving of an Oscar.

"We have an amazing menu for you this evening, which includes ingredients from across the world. We'll begin with an amuse bouche, a beef tartare, topped with a chimichurri." He paused long enough to rub his flat stomach, which Richard took to mean they could expect something delicious. He focused on the hand gestures since the words meant next to nothing to him.

Luca went on, "We'll then continue with an appetizer of crab cakes accompanied by a caper cream and a roasted red pepper remoulade. Following that, will be a lobster bisque garnished with creme fresh. So rich you'll simply want to swim in it!"

"Oh, I love the bisque!" the lady in purple exclaimed.

The waiter winked at her. "This evening, your main course will be a center cut fillet of beef with a Bordelaise and grilled asparagus. The chef is going to send out some other accompaniments, as well, and you're going to love each one more than the next. My favorite is the garlic mashed potatoes."

Ah! Now he had Richard's attention. Steak and veggies, he understood.

The tall, skinny, stick of a man wrapped up his speech. "When you're all done with that, you must visit the dessert bar. It's a taste of heaven. The champagne strawberries in creme anglaise are to die for."

He flounced away and Ike arrived out of nowhere—an impressive feat for a guy that took up as much space as two average men. "Are we having fun? Getting to know one another?"

"Not yet," the lady in purple said, leering at Richard. "I sure am looking forward to introductions, though."

"Simply fantastic," Ike said, eyes on Stanley. "Do give me a wave if there is anything at all I can do for you."

"We should introduce ourselves." The kid with the girl stuck to his arm had a voice like Beaver Cleaver—kind of looked like him, too, with his fish-belly white skin and floppy brown hair. "I'm Terry Cadwallader. This is my bright, beautiful, talented, smoking hot bride, Val."

The girl next to him rolled her eyes and swatted at him. "Oh, stop." She turned her pretty smile on the group and flipped her glossy dark hair over her shoulder. "It's very nice to meet you all. We're from Portland. This is our honeymoon. Where is everyone else from?" She fidgeted in her seat like a restless child with twinkling eyes and bright spots of color in her cheeks.

As if the person in charge of the seating chart were performing an exercise in opposites, the old lady on the girl's left had short-cropped white hair, wrinkly, pale white skin, pale blue eyes and wore a cream-colored dress. The seating effect gave one the impression that all life and color slowly drained from one woman into the other. "We live in southern Arizona. My name is Annie, Annie Santos." She jabbed a thumb in the direction of her companion—a large man the approximate shape and color of a russet potato, freshly dug from the earth. "He's Ed. We run a bed and breakfast and, I have to tell you, I couldn't be happier to have someone washing my linens and fetching my drinks for a change."

Ed Santos sat with his arms folded across his broad chest like two iron bands wrapped around an old whiskey barrel. "Speaking of drinks, they bringin' them soon?"

Annie patted his arm and answered in the sweet, high voice one would use to coax a puppy to come get his treat, "There's water on the table, dear, and we just had drinks in the bar." She forced a giggle, fake as a three-dollar bill.

He harrumphed in her direction.

What a grump, Richard thought.

As if summoned by the man's question, Luka returned, balancing a tray full of glasses and passed drinks out around the table. When he'd finished, he presented a basket of breadsticks with the flourish of a circus magician pulling a rabbit from his hat. "A treat to hold you over, yes?" He confirmed that everyone had what they needed and left again.

"I suppose that makes it my turn," the old lady in purple said. "I'm Julia Domina. I do love a good cruise, among other things." She stared into the depths of Richard's soul. "And I'm very passionate about the things I enjoy. Do tell us all about you, sir." One bejeweled hand reached for her martini glass.

Richard swallowed the lump in his throat. "I'm Dick," he said. *What? Wait! No! He hated being called Dick!* "Richard. My name is Richard. Please call me Richard. I don't like Dick."

She arched an eyebrow in his direction. "Duly noted."

"I'm a grandpa. Her grandpa." He jerked a thumb in Burke's direction. "My wife died a long time ago." He wondered why he was still talking, despite his fierce desire to stop. Thank God, the kid rescued him.

"My name is Burke. It's a pleasure to make your acquaintance, all of you. My grandfather and I and our dear friend, Stanley, all work together. We've had a wild few months, so we thought a bit of R and R was exactly what the doctor ordered."

"You all work together? That's fantastic!" Terry leaned in toward Burke. His wife mirrored him, keeping them in the same close proximity to one another. "What kind of work do you do?"

"We help people who've gotten in over their heads," Burke said.

At the same moment, Stanley said, "We solve problems."

And Richard told him, "We're exterminators."

Ed Santos laughed and burped. "So, you're hitmen for hire?" He used his teeth to pull a pineapple chunk off a plastic sword that had been stuck in his drink.

Burke winked at him. "Darn it. You figured us out."

Everyone laughed, and Luka showed up with another tray.

He slid a plate in front of each person. There appeared to be a tiny brain in the center of it, topped with the world's tiniest runny-yolk egg and garnished with some greens that had been pre-chewed and spit up in a semi-purposeful splatter pattern. "Enjoy!" He flashed his sharp smile and disappeared again.

"Oh, my! Doesn't this look amazing," Annie Santos exclaimed. Her husband snorted but picked up his fork without a word.

The young ones had already cleaned their plates, like good children.

Richard caught Stanley's eye.

Stanley smiled weakly. "It's not Strawberry waffles from Al's Breakfast."

"Surely ain't a burger from Murphy's," Richard shot back.

"Would you rather have fried cheese?"

Richard couldn't help grinning. " Darn right, I would. Fried cheese is a delicacy. I've seen mustard greens and opossum innards that looked better'n this."

Stanley's laughter was not as bright as it once had been, but hearing him laugh boosted Richard's spirits. He shoved the plateful of brainy stuff aside. Mashed potatoes had been mentioned. He'd just wait it out until they appeared.

"Oh, Richard, do tell me you're not afraid to try new things," the creepy old lady with the jewelry said.

"Ain't afraid to try new things, but don't feel the need to stick my willie in a snapping turtle's mouth just to see what it feels like, either."

Ed Santos' laughter shook the whole table. "I like you, man. You're okay."

His wife dabbed at the corners of her mouth with her white linen napkin. "Don't make a scene." She turned her attention to Julia. "I know this seems strange, but you seem terribly familiar to me. Do I know you, somehow?

"Oh, I can't imagine that you do. I'm just a girl from the Old World, trying to make it in the new."

"No. I'm quite certain I know you from somewhere," Annie insisted.

"I'm quite certain you don't," Julia replied. The smile on her face never faltered, but something in her voice sent chills up Richard's spine. He determined that for more than one reason, Julia Domina was a woman he would never allow himself to be alone with in a room.

Terry licked the last of the nasty-looking appetizer from his fork. "What are you all planning on doing tomorrow? We'll be at sea all day, so Annie and I were thinking we'd sleep late and then hit the big water slide."

"And shop. You promised me some shopping time." Annie poked him in the ribs.

He laughed and pulled her closer. "Does my princess need spoiling?"

"I'm a queen, thank you, and yes. I do need spoiling, thank you very much."

Luka popped up again and slid a plate in front of Richard. Centered on the dish was a golden brown, deep-fried hockey puck garnished with what appeared to be a tiny corn stalk growing out of the center. Richard didn't know how he was going to spend the next day. He couldn't think that far ahead. At the moment, all he could think about were the mashed potatoes he'd been promised and the twenty-four-hour all-you-can-eat buffets he had heard so much about. If he was going to survive nearly a week on this boat, he was going to need to find some kind of substance beyond the weirdo garbage they seemed to favor in this fancy dining room.

After dinner, Burke asked if they'd like to join her for a showing of an old black and white movie in one of the smaller lounges.

Stanley turned to her. "It's a wonderful film, but I believe I'll decline this time. I'm afraid the early morning and busy day have left me rather rumpled. I'm ready to call it a night."

Ike materialized once more like a big, brown, grinning wraith. "Some of the most exciting things happen at night, you know."

"Perhaps I'll feel more adventurous tomorrow," Stanley replied.

An idea struck Richard. "Hey, Ike. You got a map of the ship? I...uh...want to explore my options for tomorrow. I can give Stanley the heads up on all the best places to go."

"I believe you'll find a map in the courtesy folder in the nightstand drawer of your room, along with a list of emergency numbers, a schedule of our itinerary, a room service menu, and several other items."

A map and room service. Perfect. He could finally get something more than mashed potatoes and strawberries in his belly, and while he ate, he'd have time to form a plan of attack. They'd be at sea the whole next day. That would be plenty of time to scour the place for signs of EMF or sulfur.

With his plan in place, Richard impatiently waited for Burke to indicate that it would be socially acceptable for them to leave the dining area.

Just as promised, he found the shiny blue binder with its laminated pages in the little drawer next to the bed. He dialed the number at the top of page seven and a man with a voice like a bullfrog answered after a single ring.

"I'd like a bacon cheeseburger, fries, cheese sticks, and the loaded nacho plate," Richard said. He told the guy to charge the food to his room and include a twenty percent tip.

"Certainly, Sir. We'll have that up to you in about thirty minutes."

"Hold on." Something else had caught Richard's eye. "You've got lemon pie?"

The bullfrog confirmed that they did.

"Gimme a slice of lemon pie, too. Don't suppose you have prune juice?"

"We do, sir."

Jiminy Christmas! This was fantastic! Why did anybody bother getting all dressed up to sit in that stupid dining room? "Bring me some of that, too." He hung up the phone and turned to the map to study while he waited. The ship boasted twelve public decks. There were also four crew decks. Those might be trickier to access, but he remained confident they'd find a way.

Around midnight, he drifted off to sleep amid a clutter of dirty dishes and scribbled notes. The Weather Channel droned on quietly while he snored. He dreamed happy dreams of bacon cheeseburgers and a disturbing dream about a rich old woman with talon-like nails that dug into his back and refused to let go.

RICHARD FOUND WAKING UP AT SEA TO BE A STRANGE AND disorienting experience. His stateroom aboard the *Diversion* wasn't so different from the many hotel rooms he'd stayed in over the past several months. All those spaces resembled one another in that they featured beds with too many pillows, little round tables with uncomfortable chairs and a tiny space for travelers to stash their luggage and meager belongings. All of that was familiar, but the constant rocking sensation combined with the unfamiliar creaks, groans, and sloshes of a vessel crossing the ocean, and the distinct lack of work to be done, left him uneasy and uncertain.

Burke knocked on the door to call him to breakfast. He was really hoping it would be something more familiar than last night's crazy dinner.

The hallways aboard the *Diversion* were a softly lit, lushly carpeted labyrinth. The three hunters walked along in single file.

A maid's cart blocked the hall. Two young women stood on either side of it, and they were too involved in a heated argument to get out of the hunters' path.

The younger woman, an exceptional beauty Richard placed in her early twenties, held a white rag in her left hand and a spray bottle in her right. She gestured wildly as she spoke. "I'm just saying, if it happens again and it happens in my section, you can count me out. I signed up to do housework not to star in some kind of live-action version of a TV crime drama."

The older woman was the same smooth-skinned beauty who'd delivered the safety lecture. Her suit was pressed and flawless. Her spine could have served as a plumb line. She spoke in the cool, soft tone of a woman determined to prove that she was not overly emotional. "Nothing has happened in your section. It's always been in the Super Suites, but that's beside the point. You were hired to clean up messes, and that's what I expect you to do. I expect you to do it well, to do it efficiently, and to do it without complaining. If you can't live up to those expectations, I am sure we'll have no trouble finding a replacement when we get back to Miami. You're not the only young lady with dreams of traveling around the world for free. Better than free, we're paying you a generous salary."

The woman in the navy-blue suit put one hand on the edge of the cart. A year ago, Richard would have noticed nothing strange about the gesture, but everything he'd seen in recent months had honed his skills of observation to an edge as sharp as a surgeon's scalpel. The woman's knuckles turned white with the pressure of her grip on the cart. The muscle along her jawline twitched as she ground her teeth. "I strongly suggest that you spend more time focusing on your duties and less time gossiping with the rest of the staff."

Burke cleared her throat and the woman jumped at the sound. An experienced hospitality professional, she arranged her features into a pleasant smile. "Excuse us. My associate and I were just moving this cart out of the way. We didn't hear anyone coming. Are you headed down to breakfast?"

"We are," Burke replied.

"Fantastic. I hear the chefs were up half the night preparing some extra special treats."

Richard groaned. He didn't want anything special. Maybe he'd be better off staying in his room and ordering bacon and eggs off the room service menu. They'd made a fine burger the night before.

"Don't mind my grandfather," Burke said in response to the woman's concerned glance. "He's a firm believer that grumbling will add years to his life."

The woman's toothy smile returned. "Well, if breakfast or anything else doesn't meet your expectations, please don't hesitate to let me know. I'll put a word in for you and see what we can do about improving your experience. It's our goal to make sure this is the happiest voyage of your life so far. My extension is programmed into your room phone under the concierge button. My name is Nikki. Or you can speak with my associate here anytime. Isabelle's your designated room steward."

Without a word, Isabelle shoved the cart into the nearest stateroom.

Burke lead Richard and Stanley past the women to the elevator.

"Did anything about that seem strange to you?" Richard asked.

"I wouldn't say strange so much as uncomfortable. It sounds like young Isabelle is having a rough go of it," Burke replied.

"What do you think she meant about her job being like something out of a TV crime drama?"

Burke shrugged. "Who knows?"

Richard wondered if he'd already found his first clue. He turned to Stanley. "Ain't you got nothing to say about anything anymore?"

Stanley conjured a joyless little grin. "The world is full of strange things, Richard. I'm too old and too weary to chase after each and every one of them."

"You didn't have a problem with it a few months ago." Richard immediately wished he could pull the words back into himself. He didn't mean to wound Stanley. Not really. He only wanted to see the man's former spark flare. This listless old man disturbed him. This version of Stanley was too similar to himself when he was shut away in the old folks' home. Better dead than wasting away like that again.

At the thought, he shivered. Stanley couldn't give up and go over to the reaper. Not yet. Not from old age. Stanley needed to go down with a gun in each hand and take an army of monsters with him.

Richard set the conversation between the women on a back burner to let it simmer for a while. Excitement stirred in his heart. He'd been right! Something fishy was happening on the *Diversion* and he and Stanley were going to figure out what it was.

The hunt was on.

But first...breakfast.

BREAKFAST MADE UP FOR DINNER. THE BUFFET TABLE stretched the length of a football field, or so it seemed to Richard's delighted eyes. His stomach roared like a lion announcing its intentions to hunt on the open savannah. His mouth watered. He swallowed hard and hitched his pants up a notch. "I'll meet you at the table. I'm going to the other end. They always put the fancy pastries and meat last so you'll have less room on your plate and take less, but I know their tricks."

He hustled away before either of his skinny companions could tell him about how all the best things in life will kill you. What's the point of living if you're half-starved to distraction all the time and filled up on stuff that tastes like overripe gym socks the rest of the time? Besides, he'd already had more than eight decades. Everything in the future counted as bonus days.

The sturdy white plate he grabbed off the rolling cart still radiated heat from the dishwasher. He carried it to the line and slipped in at the end of the long table between a woman half a foot taller and twice as wide as him and a man dragging an oxygen tank behind him. "'Scuse me," he mumbled as he reached for a fat cinnamon roll.

"No worries," the man with the oxygen tank said. He scooped a good half-rasher of bacon out of the tub and put it on his plate. "Doctor said cholesterol'll kill me. I told him, 'Least I'll die happy.'"

"I figure any extra calories I put on from eating, I'll burn walking around the tourist traps when we land," the woman said.

Richard wondered if he could request that these reasonable folks replace some of his current dinnertime tablemates.

After fighting his way upstream against the current of fools who started at the end with the fruit and boiled eggs, he carried his heavily laden plate to the table where Burke and Richard were already seated. He plopped a donut and a slab of ham next to Stanley's scoop of cottage cheese with peaches on top. "Eat something. You're gettin' too skinny."

The corner of Stanley's mouth twitched. "Your concern is overwhelming, Dick."

Lord, but Richard hated being called Dick, and Stanley knew it. He debated if he should smile because Stanley still had enough gumption to be a complete ninny, or if he should declare offense at the insult. In the end, he settled for jamming a sausage in his mouth. Hot grease carried the strong flavor of sage over his tongue and everything else blurred to background noise for the duration of the meal.

BURKE WANTED TO GO TO THE GYM. WHY PEOPLE WENT ON vacation, saying they wanted to relax, and then spent their time chasing the wind on a treadmill, Richard would never understand. At least, she didn't try to talk him into joining her. He detested fitness evangelists.

"Let's check things out," he said to Stanley.

"Which things are you thinking of checking?" Stanley asked.

"I brought my EMF detector." Richard pulled the little square box from his pocket and held it up.

Stanley's brows tilted downward. "Why?"

"Why? Did you hear what those girls were saying? There's something hinky going on on this ship and we're going to find out what it is."

Stanley leaned on his cane with both hands. "I don't know, Dick. I think I'd like to—"

Richard cut him off, "I won't take no for an answer. Come on, old man." He stalked off toward the rear of the ship and let Stanley catch up.

Once they'd crossed the lobby and entered the long quiet halls lined with doors that opened onto guest rooms, Stanley asked, "Do you even know where you're going?"

Richard harrumphed. "The girl said whatever happened, happened in the Super Suites. I'm pretty sure those rooms are toward the back of the boat, a deck or two higher up than our rooms."

Stanley raised no further objections. Richard kept an eye on the EMF while they walked, but the only tiny blips that registered were those you'd expect from electrical interference that came when they passed equipment rooms.

As they drew closer to the stern, the doors to the cabins became fewer and farther between.

Stanley cleared his throat. "I don't think—"

"There are all kinds of monsters that don't emit EMF," Richard said. "Maybe we should—"

"Richard, I know you—"

Richard turned to face Stanley. He held up the detector. "Honestly, could be that the batteries are dead. I meant to change them and I forgot. Shoot a monkey, if my head wasn't attached, I'd need wood screws."

"Richard, really—"

Richard noticed one door had been propped so it wouldn't latch. "Look. This one's open." He pushed past Stanley and opened the door wide. A rainbow of roses covered every flat surface in the room. Red and white petals lay scattered across the thick white bedspread. The sweet heady fragrance of the flowers drifted out of the room.

Stanley staggered back as if someone had punched him. His pale face turned a sickly shade of gray. "We need to go." He tripped backward two or three steps down the hallway. "Close the door, Richard. We have to go. We have to go now."

Richard scowled. "What in tarnation's wrong with you?"

Stanley shook his head back and forth in short, jerking motions. "We need to get out of here. I need to get out of here." He turned and started limping down the hall, his cane thumping hard against the carpeted floor.

"Stanley!" Richard called. "Stan Kapcheck, what's wrong with you? You gonna just leave me standing here with my detector in my hand?"

"I need to go," Stanley called back in the instant before he disappeared around a corner in the hallway.

Richard looked back into the room. On the mirror, someone had scrawled, *Will you marry me?* He sighed and pulled the door shut again, careful not to engage the latch.

"What the devil got into you, Stanley?" he muttered. Then it came to him. The Devil. Every time The Devil appeared in all her blonde-haired, long-legged glory, she carried the scent of roses with her. "Crap on a cracker." He jammed the EMF detector into his pocket and stumped along the hall. He'd be forced to admit to Burke that his idea went down a hill and off a cliff from there. He threw the door to the lobby open and stood there, trying to figure out where to go next. It wasn't even ten o'clock yet—still almost three hours until lunch. What the heck was he supposed to do until then?

A flat-screen television mounted on the wall in front of him flashed a picture of the waterslide as if making a suggestion.

"Over my cold dead body," he said.

A woman passing by made a wide berth around him.

Richard stuck his tongue out at her back.

The picture on the TV switched to an advertisement for a sports bar on deck four. Maybe they'd show clips from the game he missed the night before. Better than sitting in his closet of a room alone, he figured, and slumped off toward the big glass elevator.

CHAPTER FIVE

Burke

THE RHYTHM OF HER FEET SLAPPING THE TREADMILL'S WIDE belt sent Burke into a near-hypnotic trance. Running, she could empty her mind of doubt and fear, anger, hurt, all the garbage and baggage that threatened to drag a person down in life. Oxygen, pulled into her body, used up, released, pulled in again, became the only important thing in existence. In front of her, beyond the tinted glass of the ship's gym, the ocean stretched to infinity. She could run forever, or until she slipped off the edge of the Earth and floated away into the Milky Way.

Her legs burned under the strain. She turned the speed up a notch and ran faster, eyes straight ahead, arms pumping at her sides. Another minute. Five. Ten. Finally, she gave in to her exhaustion and pressed the button that would allow the machine to slow to a stop.

She grabbed a towel from the shelf to mop sweat from her face. Now that her feet stood still, her mind resumed its usual chatter. Something had to be done about Stanley. So far,

Stanley seemed the same. They needed to get him involved. He had to remember how to have fun. Clearly, the gym held no appeal for him, but maybe he'd enjoy the pool. If his leg hurt, the buoyancy of the water might help, and if he didn't feel like swimming, laying in the sun had to be therapeutic, right?

Armed with a plan, albeit a fairly pathetic plan, she breezed through the gym door and crashed into Captain Northrup.

"I'm so sorry."

He placed a steadying hand on her arm. "No. Forgive me. It was my fault. Are you enjoying your voyage so far?"

Burke wondered what he would suggest to engage someone who'd existed for a short time as nothing but goodness and light, and then resumed the burden of darkness that was the curse of humanity. Did the bar mix a special cocktail for that? She settled for telling him that everything had been lovely. "I figure, if I run a few miles every day, I don't have to feel so guilty about that dessert bar at dinner."

His laugh brought to mind the game show hosts she'd watched on television as a child. "My dear, haven't you heard? Cruise calories don't count."

"I wonder if all this luxury and indulgence ever becomes boring to you."

"Boring? No." His attention seemed to drift far away. "Not boring. I'd say there were simpler, more enjoyable times, though."

She waited for him to say more.

He gave a slight shake of his head, and the wide, white smile returned. "Listen to me. I sound like an old man remembering yesteryear, don't I? Well, none of that. I'll let you continue on your way. You take care to have fun, and make sure to take a second helping tonight at dinner." He nodded toward the gym door. "You earned it."

Burke mused about his words as she walked along the quiet passageways. What would lessen enjoyment of captaining a cruise ship? Political red tape, because they crossed international waters so frequently? Too many entitled passengers expecting special favors?

She knocked on Stanley's door and waited so long for him to answer she almost gave up, on the assumption he'd gone off with her grandfather. When he answered, at last, his shirttail hung untucked from his pants and the big toe of his left foot stuck out of a large hole in his sock.

Burke fought the tears that threatened. The Stanley she knew would have sooner died than answer the door in such a disheveled state. She plastered the biggest smile she could muster across her face. "I'm going to change and head up to the pool. Would you like to join me?"

Stanley ran a hand across the smooth skin of his scalp. "Oh, no. I'm not sure I'm—"

"I hear that water is fantastic for aching joints, and sunshine makes everything better."

He lifted one bony shoulder. "I appreciate the invitation. I think I'd like to lie down for a time. I'm feeling a touch thin around the edges."

No description could have been more fitting. Burke swallowed hard. "I'll come back and get you when we go to lunch."

"Perhaps you should wait until dinner."

Burke nodded. "Sure, Stanley. Dinner. I'll see you then."

He closed the door gently, but the click of the latch made her jump as if he'd slammed it with all his might.

Thin around the edges, indeed.

Dejected, sad, tired from running, and feeling directionless, she changed into her favorite bright green bathing suit and tied the matching wrap around her waist. Ten minutes later, she was settling into a lounge chair with soft white cushions. She ordered a drink from a girl with a glossy blonde ponytail and a tan that gave her skin the luster of freshly processed leather. The Dan Brown novel she'd brought with her gave off a fantastic new book smell. Her spirits began to lift, and she determined to try again ASAP to get Stanley to join her poolside.

A shadow fell across the pages of her book. "Excuse me, but I have to ask. Did it hurt?"

Burke looked up at the man standing over her. With the sun behind him, he was little more than a shadow. She scrambled to her feet, ready to fight.

He held up his hands in surrender. "I didn't mean to startle you." He stood maybe five feet, four inches tall, but his Afro gave him another half a foot. His voice was soft and smooth and captivating. He wore a bright purple Speedo and a red and purple silk robe with the ties loose at the sides. A large gold chain lay across his thin, hairless chest.

She pressed a hand to her pounding heart. "I thought you were...someone else." Memories of the attacking shadow demons wrenched a shiver from her.

He lowered his sunglasses and peered at her above the rims. "I am no one else and no one else will ever be the one and only Isaac Barrera."

"Sorry." How many times would she have to apologize in one day?

"I never hold a grudge. May I join you?"

Burke showed him her book. "I'm not much company right now. I have a date with Mr. Brown."

Isaac settled into the lounge chair next to hers. The silk

robe pooled on the wooden deck on either side of him. He folded his hands across his stomach.

Burke rolled her eyes, dropped back down into her own chair, and opened her book.

"Do you cruise often?" he asked.

She stared at the pages in front of her. "First time."

"Oh! A virgin!" He giggled. "I myself am a traveling man. I've crossed the ocean more often than a great white shark. I don't bite though." He leaned toward her. "Unless you want me to."

"No, thank you," Burke said through clenched teeth. The Eagles started singing "Witchy Woman." She snatched up the phone and looked at the display. It presented a unique quandary: Remain stuck in a conversation with an idiot who couldn't take a hint, or use the call as an exit, and end up stuck in a conversation with an idiot who couldn't take a hint.

A shared history and morbid curiosity won out. "Excuse me," she told the small man with the big hair. She slid her thumb across the green circle as she stood up and wandered toward the deck rail. "What do you need?"

Her ex-husband's deep, sexy voice crooned in her ear, "Why do you always assume I need something?"

"History repeats," she said.

"Aw, Bebe. Don't be that way."

Heat unfurled in her belly, and she hated him for causing that reaction. Stupid traitorous body. "I'm not your Bebe. Why are you calling me? I thought you were at an ashram in Colorado."

He hesitated a beat—probably needed time to get his story in order. "I left."

She wandered down the deck, dragging her left hand along the smooth railing. "Did they kick you out?"

"I chose to leave."

"They kicked you out."

"They didn't kick me out. I left voluntarily."

To give credit where credit was due, he must have learned something at the ashram, because back in the days when they'd been husband and wife, he'd have blown his top by now. This new super Zen Greg remained freakishly calm. Perhaps he'd partaken of the good old Rocky Mountain High during his time in Colorado. "All right," Burke said. "I'll bite. Why did you decide to leave?"

"I went there to grow as a person. Eventually, I outgrew the teacher."

Burke realized she'd left her drink behind, and there was no getting it back without getting past Little Romeo. The lack of a good strong drink counted as one of life's mundane tragedies. "The teacher must have been small."

Greg's deep breathing was audible over the phone. "Why must you push my buttons, Bebe?"

She snorted. "Maybe because you insist on calling me Bebe. Maybe because you made me feel small and stupid and insignificant when I should have felt like queen of the world. Then again, to be honest, I'm pretty sure it's mostly because you cheated on me."

"I understand those things upset you, and I forgive you for your anger."

Her anger was quickly heating up to full-on rage. She gripped the railing so tight her hand ached. "Why did you call me?"

"I really did want to talk to you, to see how you're doing."

"Uh huh. That's why you've asked about my wellbeing."

"Well, there's something else that I suppose distracted me."

She rolled her eyes. "I'm stunned."

"Seriously, Be...uh...Burke. I think I might be in trouble."

"Did your latest hook up put out a contract on you?"

He made a weird noise like he was choking. Crying? Was he capable of that level of emotion? "I don't know." He sniffed. "It could be. I don't think so. I...I just don't know."

He'd thrown her. She hadn't literally thought that some woman might have put a contract out on him. She could relate to wanting him dead on a meta level, but to take real action... that took next level anger. What had he done to the poor girl? "Why do you think someone's following you?"

"I can't say, exactly. It's like I have this super creepy feeling. I see things out of the corner of my eye, and when I look there's nothing there. My stuff moves."

The back of her neck tingled. "Your stuff?"

He sniffed again. "Yeah. Like, I put my wallet on the nightstand at the hotel. I know I did. It couldn't have been anywhere else because I remember getting my credit card out to order pizza. This morning it was next to the sink."

"You probably—"

"I didn't move it!"

So much for Zen.

"And that's not all. I feel weird. Something malevolent has it out for me. I know it."

A couple in matching neon orange tracksuits power-walked past Burke. She tapped her fingernails against the railing. She'd promised herself a thousand times to never let Greg suck her into his personal drama again. A cloud passed in front of the sun, casting the deck into shadow. Burke shivered in the sudden cool.

"Bebe?"

"Don't," she warned.

"You were quiet a long time," he said.

She chewed on her bottom lip.

"Do you believe me?"

Lord Almighty, above, she did, but with all her heart she wished she didn't. Rather than confess her belief to her adulterous ex, she asked, "Where are you?"

"I'm still in Colorado, but heading south toward New Mexico. I heard there are some fantastic spiritual communities around Santa Fe. Well...near Santa Fe, outside of a little town called Tesuque."

"Spiritual communities?" she asked.

His voice returned to the familiar sexy baritone, "I've told you. I've changed."

His words reminded her of how far she'd come in the past year. After a decade of moping around with no clear purpose, she'd found a place in the world where she felt strong, where she was confident that she was making a difference. "Haven't we all," she agreed. "Look, Greg. I'm not sure what you want me to do for you."

"I guess I wanted someone to know where I was. You know...just in case. I couldn't think of anyone else to call."

Again, that brief jolt of electric fear made her gut tighten. She embraced it, preferring fear rather than pity. "All right. Let me know when you get there, okay?"

"Yeah. Okay. I figure I should be there day after tomorrow. Maybe the day after that, if I stop anywhere."

She navigated the choppy waters of goodbyes that no longer included I love you.

The sun burned through the meager cloud cover and shed its warmth on her again. The smooth waves failed to negate the wild storm of emotion churning inside her. Greg had lied and cheated and belittled her. He deserved whatever he got.

Hunters are led to their hunts, Stanley said in her mind.

It's not a hunt. It's only Greg, trying to suck me back into his world because he's lonely.

Her fingernails clicked against the railing.

Finally, she lifted her phone and scrolled through the contacts. She'd been to Santa Fe not so long ago. It wouldn't hurt to make one call. The number she dialed rang four times and clicked over to a robotic voice telling her to leave a message.

"Nathaniel, this is Stanley Kapcheck's friend, Burke. I have a favor to ask. An acquaintance of mine just called, and he's heading your way. He says he's going to try to hook up with some kind of spiritual community in the area near Tesuque, but he's got a feeling there's some bad mojo on his tail. I was wondering if you could keep an ear out for me. His name is Greg Martin. He'll be there in two or three days. I know it's not a lot to go on, but if you hear of anything strange, please give me a call. Thanks."

She clicked the phone off and rolled her eyes. Freakin' Greg. He'd sucked up enough of her mental energy for one day.

CHAPTER SIX

Gordon

GORDON SAT AT THE PLAIN METAL DESK IN HIS CLOSET-LIKE office filling out paperwork about a missing diamond earring. The complainant was the eighty-seven-year-old wife of a retired banking executive. She'd woken up in the morning, removed her jewelry bag from her suitcase for the first time since boarding the ship, found the earring missing, and immediately reported it stolen, blaming everyone from the customs officials to the room steward when, clearly, she'd only packed one earring to begin with. Still, a complaint meant the paperwork had to be filed. His job was nothing if not glamorous.

The phone on his desk rang and he snatched it up before the first sound had time to fade away. "Westchester."

"Chief Westchester, this is Nora from the infirmary."

The pencil in his hand snapped in half. "Where?"

She cited a suite number and he was off and running before he heard another word.

He slowed to a brisk trot when he passed through the

more populated areas of the ship. What's the hurry? Can't save the dead.

The ship's doctor and one of her assistants stood hunched over the body. Ike huddled in the corner with eyes the size of saucers and his hand over his mouth. The new kid from Brazil stood guard at the door. Gordon passed by. "Same as the others?"

They'd been down this road so many times lately, long explanations and minute details were no longer required. The doctor nodded and stepped back to let Gordon see.

A man—white-haired, big-bellied, and fully clothed—lay on the bed, arms and legs akimbo, eyes wide open, smiling like Jezabel herself just walked through the door.

Gordon swallowed hard. "It could be a germ, some kind of bacteria."

In the corner, the activities director made a weird little moan of despair.

"We've been down this road, Gordon. This is cardiac arrest and there is nothing I know that could do this. I even called a friend who works at the CDC—"

"You alerted the Center for Disease control that there's a possible lethal contaminant on this ship?"

The Brazilian kid stepped back.

"Calm down, would you? I didn't say I called the CDC. I said I called a friend who works for the CDC. He agreed. It's straight-up heart failure."

Gordon peered down at the happy corpse. "Except it's not."

The doctor nodded. "Yeah. Except for that."

He heaved a sigh and then spoke in his command voice, "Y'all know the drill. Seal the crime scene. Get a guard on the end of the hall. No one comes in or out unless they belong here. Last thing we need is some curious old geezer down here looking for sick kicks. And keep it quiet. No one knows, you hear me? No one finds out about this without my permission. I don't care if it's the President himself.

"Ike, you go out there and make sure this is the most satisfied group of humans that ever floated on the sea. Keep them busy and guarantee no one has so much as a hangnail to complain about.

"Doc, I want all the info you can give me this side of a criminal violation and maybe just a little on the other side."

"Is it a bacteria? Could we get sick?" Tears swam in the young officer's eyes. "I just met this girl. She works in the salon and I don't want to make her sick."

"Son, far as I can tell, you're safe until your income triples and your curlies turn white. Now, I suggest you get on the radio and do as I say or you're gonna wish a fatal contagion was your worst concern."

"Yes, sir."

Gordon rolled his eyes and hoped to God there was any kind of clue at this crime scene because the last dozen had left him absolutely nowhere.

CHAPTER SEVEN

Richard

RICHARD NEVER MADE IT TO THE SPORTS BAR. HALFWAY there, he bumped into Ed and Annie Santos.

"You should come play shuffleboard with us!" Annie exclaimed.

He stuffed his hands in his pockets. "Nah. Thanks, though. I don't want to intrude."

"Heh, heh, heh," a chuckle rumbled up and out of Ed's barrel chest. "Ain't no game going on there. Buncha old farts sitting around the edges of the painted lines killing what's left of their livers and healthy skin cells."

When you put it that way, it sounded better than sitting alone in a dark bar. He agreed with a shrug. Annie clapped her hands in delight and led them along, chattering like a tour guide.

Ed studied him while they walked.

"What?" Richard asked. Being stared at was downright irritating.

"Why you always so grumpy?" Ed asked.

"What?"

"You look like you swallowed a sour pickle you forgot to chew. Why you so grumpy?"

Richard harrumphed. Who did the big galoot think he was, getting into his personal business? "I ain't grumpy. Just don't go around all day grinning like an idiot."

Ed walked in long, loping steps with his hands in his pockets. "You oughta smoke a joint. It'd calm you down."

Richard's blood pressure shot up. "I don't need drugs to calm down!"

A group of fat old women in flower print bathing suits with matching skirts shot alarmed glances in their direction and made a wide berth around them.

"Think maybe you do," Ed replied in his slow drawl. "You're wound so tight your mainspring's gonna pop. A hit on a doobie'd do you good. Might save you from an ulcer."

The exceptionally large breakfast churned uncomfortably in Richard's stomach. "You don't know nothing about my guts. Ain't right to go assuming things about a man. All kinds of things about me you don't know. I'm fit as a fiddle and finer than frog's hair, thank you very much."

Ed bellowed with laughter. "I like you, man. Gotta get you a golden ticket."

Richard stomped along and wondered how big the freaking ship could be. How much farther were they going to walk? Where was this stupid shuffleboard court and why was he headed there with these weirdos anyway?

The big man kept talking, even though no one had asked him to. "You see, I met a guy once. Told me about an alien planet with purple clouds. Said that's the real Heaven. Ain't some mystical dimension, just another planet on the other side of another galaxy." This observation provoked another round of rumbling chuckles. "Turns out, according to this guy, we weren't created by an old white dude with a long beard, but a little green man from outer space." He shrugged his wide, sloped shoulders as if to say, who am I to question? "Little green man promised he'd come back some day after we crawled up out of the muck and learned how to bang two rocks together to make a fire. He's gonna fly us away to his purple-cloud planet, but not all of us. Just the ones smart enough to know what's up. Gotta have a ticket."

Richard pressed his lips together and refrained from comment. The man was obviously nutty as a squirrel turd.

"So, the guy asked me if I wanted a golden ticket. I told him I surely did." With a bit of grunting and huffing Ed dug a battered brown wallet from the pocket of his ill-fitting short pants and produced from it a yellow piece of paper with the words: This Golden Ticket Implies Belief In The Great Supreme Ones And Their Ultimate Master Plan And Entitles The Carrier To One Free Ride Aboard A Starship To The Planet Of Purple Clouds And Pleasure. (No refunds, exchanges, or round-trip accommodations provided.)

Richard read it and passed it back. All by themselves, his eyes rolled. He couldn't have stopped them if his life had depended on it.

Of course, Ed chuckled at his reaction. "It's a load of crap, obviously. The guy who gave it to me was crazier than an outhouse rat." He tucked the ticket back into his wallet and stuffed the whole thing into his pocket again. "Still, I don't wanna take any chances. I figure I'll carry it with me. Just in case."

"I just remembered. I'm supposed to find Burke," Richard lied.

Annie pointed ahead. "She's right there, dear."

Burke caught his eye and gave a little wave. She stood near the railing with her phone clutched in her hand.

"We're going to get drunk next to the shuffleboard court," Annie told her once they'd gotten close enough to speak without shouting.

Richard expected a comment about healthy living, but Burke only nodded. "That's the best idea I've heard all day."

"That ain't saying much," Ed said. "It ain't even noon yet."

"It's five o'clock somewhere," Burke replied.

Ed gestured toward Burke and told Richard, "I like her, too."

Richard wondered how he'd ended up on a boat surrounded by crazy people.

Two shuffleboard courts were painted onto the wooden deck near the bow of the ship. No one played on either, but a dozen or so old folks reclined in the cushioned chairs. Several of them sipped drinks that held umbrellas, swords, or long colorful sticks. One fat man with a thick mat of wiry white hair bristling from his chest snored peacefully. Annie suggested they sit at one of the glass-topped tables. The moment their backsides touched the thick-cushioned, high-backed chairs, Luca and Ike popped up out of thin air, side-by-side, grinning at them like two sharks that had jumped out of the water and landed on the ship by happy accident.

"Good morning! It is a beautiful day, no? We have wonderful treats for you!" Luca clapped his bony hands in front of his thin chest.

"Are we having a fabulous time?" Ike asked.

"Oh, we are, yes," Annie said, pressing one hand across her heart.

"Where's Mr. Kapcheck this morning?"

Ed chuckled.

"He's resting in his room," Burke said. "I'm sure he'll be out later."

"May I bring you something to drink?" Luca bounced on his toes as if on the verge of bursting from hopeful expectation. No one had ever wanted to fetch drinks as badly as this young man wanted to fetch drinks. He was the golden retriever of the high seas.

"I'll have a mimosa, dear," Annie said.

"Excellent choice," Luca replied.

Burke ordered a Bloody Mary. Ed asked for scotch and soda.

Breakfast gurgled with all the clatter of a backed-up sump pump in Richard's gut. The last thing he needed was hard liquor. "Can I get a glass of soda water with ice?"

Luca spread his long, lanky arms wide. "Of course!"

"Really living the high life, eh, Dick?" Ed jabbed him in the ribs with an elbow as pointy as a porcupine pecker.

Richard would have made a very snappy retort, but Ike interrupted, "I hope you take full advantage of what the *Diversion* can offer you today, folks. Whether it's dance lessons in the ballroom or a plunge down our waterslide, we have amusements for everyone." He said the polite things a person's expected say before exiting a conversation and then moved on to another group.

The overly solicitous server brought everyone's drinks as well as a basket of snack mix.

Annie took a sip from her champagne glass and declared she had a bit of news to share.

"So, you all remember last night when I said that Julia Domina seemed familiar to me?" She waited for their nods of agreement. "Well, after dinner, we went back to our room and

I couldn't sleep because *someone* was snoring very loudly." She shot a look at Ed.

Ed stared out at the sea.

Annie went on, "I went on my Facebook page. My grandson set it up for me so we could keep in touch. He's a student at Brown University. He's in the engineering program there. Anyway, I searched Julia Domina, thinking maybe she was a friend of a friend, but what came up was an article I read some time back. It turns out Ms. Domina is somewhat famous for choosing to retire aboard this ship."

"She lives here?" Burke asked.

"That's right," Annie confirmed. "She's been cruising on the *Diversion* for more than two years now. Before that, she was on another ship with another cruise line, but they went defunct or some such thing, and so she was forced to move on. She said in the interview that she did the math and it cost no more to live on this ship than it cost to live in a well-appointed retirement community. Plus, here, the dining options are endless. She said she's a real people person, and it brings her great joy to see a whole new world of neighbors coming aboard every week."

"Wow. That's a unique way of looking at things, but I can't deny it sort of makes sense," Burke said. "I mean, why not, right?"

Annie shook her head. "I think it's strange. There's something about it...about the instability and all the constant activity. It seems unnatural."

Richard drank his soda and stayed quiet. The old bat didn't know *unnatural*. He could tell her some stories.

Ed shook the tumbler in his hand, making the ice cubes clink with a sound like tin spiders skittering across glass. "I bet that old broad gets more action with these rich old farts than a frat boy whose Daddy owns a brewery."

"You're disgusting," Annie told him.

"Yet here you are," he replied with a laugh.

Richard squinted against the glare of the sun. The hairs on his neck itched and bristled, and not just from too much coconut-scented sunscreen. Ed's words poked his reptile brain awake, but he couldn't nail down why. He lay his head back and watched a puffy white cloud in the shape of a dragon glide along behind a thin gray wisp with a weasel-shaped head. The sun shone through the glass table and warmed his legs. He replayed Annie's gossip on the warbling recorder of his mind and shivered. Why was he shivering? The marrow of his bones warmed and softened under the tropical sky.

"I'VE WAITED A LONG TIME FOR YOU," JULIA SAID. HER husky voice riled him up, or maybe it was the white silk negligee that poured like water from her feminine curves. He reached up and tried to pat his poofy hair into some semblance of a style. The time had come to make his move. It had been a real long time since he started that engine, but he knew for sure it would roar to life once he turned the key. He took a step toward her, but Luca stepped forward and blocked his path.

"I beg you to let me tell you of the glorious feast that awaits." He reached left and grasped the handle of a shiny metal cart. It rolled toward them. One faulty wheel rattled and Richard's mind filled with images of striking rattlesnakes.

Snakes. He stood in a seething mass of snakes. He stumbled backward trying to get out of the hissing, coiling nest, but it stretched interminably in every direction.

Julia winked at him and slid one arm out of the tiny ribbon that served as a strap. "I find you terribly intriguing, Richard."

The snakes merged and grew in size, no longer a nest of thousands, but a single creature—the bowrow he and Stanley fought in North Dakota.

They'd passed through customs before boarding the ship, so Richard had been forced to leave all his weapons behind. "Help me!" he shouted at Luca, but the server was gone.

Ike and Captain Northrup wandered into his field of vision.

The activities director towered over him. "Having a nice voyage?"

"Looks like you're getting some good action there." The captain chuckled and elbowed his co-worker.

"I'm in big trouble. Help me." Richard didn't feel guilty about whining. The bowrow lifted itself up high, ready to strike. Its scaly little arms waved in the air. The tips of its claws sparkled like cut glass.

Julia's negligée slipped down the length of her body and pooled around her feet. Her milky skin shone in the silver light of the moon.

Terry and Val Cadwallader popped up behind Julia. Terry embraced his young wife and then turned red, glowing eyes on Richard. "Feed the beast, Richard. You only live once."

The bowrow struck and he jumped back, crashing into Stanley. "Thank God you're here!" Richard said, but when he looked at Stan, the man's skin turned gray and blew away from his bones, no more than cold ash in a hot desert wind.

RICHARD JOLTED AWAKE WITH A SHOUT.

Ed's low laugh rolled over him like a dump truck full of manure.

He blinked and looked around. Ed and Annie and Burke watched him.

"You okay?" Burke asked.

He ran a shaky hand through his hair. "Yeah," he told her. "I'm fine. I just dozed off." But the memory of the dream was a naked mole rat burrowing into his mind. What was he missing? He needed to figure it out before someone on the ship died.

AT THE DINNER TABLE THAT NIGHT, VALERIE PULLED herself out of her husband's grasping tentacles long enough to apologize for their endless canoodling. Her eyes twinkled with the glee of a person who knew something shocking. "Did you hear one of the passengers died earlier today? That's probably why Ike looks so done-in."

Richard's fork clattered against his plate.

Burke shot him a look. "What happened?" she asked.

"I don't know, but apparently it's not the first time."

Julia waved a dismissive hand. The topaz gems on her fingers cast tiny lightning bolts of reflection toward the dining room ceiling. "Cruise ships are infested with old people. Old people die."

"Well, apparently more of them die on this cruise line than any other. So many that some people are starting to say they're going to go bankrupt," Terry supplied.

The pasta in Richard's stomach turned to lead. He knew it! He knew their next hunt was right under their noses. He'd told

Burke as much half a dozen times, most recently less than an hour before.

After his naptime nightmare, he'd excused himself and wandered every which way until he found a little library among the ship's lower decks. Conditioned air chilled the small space that smelled of dusty paper and ink. Stained glass shades cast their light over the backs of leather chairs with brass studs. The only other occupant of the room was a sulky-looking teenage girl curled up in a corner with a romance novel. She never even peeked past the veil of her mousy brown hair to see who else had come in. He knew at once he'd found the best spot on the boat. He settled in with a copy of Norman Mailer's *The Fight*, and by page ten he'd drifted into a sound and dreamless sleep.

When he woke up, he looked at his watch, realized he'd missed lunch, and decided to return to his room to order another burger. By the time it came and he finished it, Burke was knocking on his door to remind him he needed to dress nice for dinner. He informed her that he was not a child and didn't need her to dress him and then he changed out of the baggy knit shirt he'd intended to wear into a clean white t-shirt and a button down. As he dressed, he reflected on the fact that this trip really did seem to be revolving entirely around mealtimes.

Burke came back and he said as much to her.

"Are you complaining?" she asked.

"No. Just stating the facts. If we keep eating like this, we're gonna get fat as ticks on a bloodhound."

She leaned forward to check her lipstick in the mirror over his dresser. "You could work out with me, burn some of those calories."

"I got better things to do than run in place for an hour. You see me running, you better run too, 'cause something bad is coming along behind me."

She rolled her eyes at him in the mirror. Her dangly golden earrings danced across her bare shoulders. She'd gotten all gussied up again in a yellow strapless sundress.

"You clean up pretty good, kid," he told her.

She hesitated a moment as if unsure whether he teased, then thanked him. "Shall we go get Stanley?"

"Yeah, sure," he said, "but first I wanna say something."

Her chin lifted a fraction of an inch. "Go ahead."

"I know you think he needs to rest, and I'll grant you that when we went exploring last time with the EMF detector—"

"You did what?" Her thin eyebrows arched higher.

Crap! He'd forgotten that she didn't know about that. "Stan and me just took a little walk to scope things out and—"

"And what did you find?"

The chilly edge to her voice froze the hairs on the back of his neck. "Nothing, really."

"And how did Stanley react to this little excursion?"

He nearly peed himself and ran like a squirrel facing a semi-truck. Richard sure as heck wasn't going to say that to Burke, though. "He was the same as he has been." There. The truth. More or less.

"So, you found nothing and Stanley stayed the same," she said.

He scowled. "Well, yeah, but I still got this weird feeling. Something's going on on this ship. We don't get to show up anywhere and have nothing happen anymore. We're hunters now. Something bigger than we understand is using us and if we get too relaxed, we're gonna miss what's right under our noses."

"We're on vacation," she told him. "God knows that

Stanley needs a break, and that's what we're doing." She made it abundantly clear that she was done talking about this and breezed through the door to go collect Stanley for dinner.

They arrived in the dining room where Ike said hello to Richard and Burke and extended a hand to Stanley.

Stanley shook.

Ike didn't let go, but clasped his jumbo-sized left paw over Stan's right. "I haven't seen you anywhere, Stanley. Tell me you're enjoying your voyage."

Stanley inclined his head. "I must admit, I was rather exhausted when I boarded this ship. I've been in bed nearly the entire time."

The big man winked. "Color me interested, Mr. Kapcheck." He released Stanley and turned them over to the hostess who, in turn, directed them to their assigned seats. The rest of the campers were already getting loaded. Ed appeared to be struggling to remain upright in his chair.

Luca bounced up to the table and rattled off a three-minute spiel. The only part Richard understood was smoked salmon Alfredo with garlic breadsticks. Quite honestly, he was still full of burger and fries, but there was always room for pasta. Of course, he had to hurdle past the little yellow and white gelatinous blob that was said to be served, "Compliments of the chef," and a salad that contained actual dandelions. If he'd wanted to eat garden weeds, he didn't need to travel halfway around the world and pay an arm and a leg to do so.

Once the real food came, Ike made a second pass by the table to be sure they were all enjoying themselves. Once he moved on, Valarie piped up with her news report.

"Where did you hear about someone dying?" Burke asked.

Terry brushed the glossy dark curls from Val's neck and

planted a lingering kiss there. "She got her hair done today and the girl was talking about it. Doesn't she look beautiful?"

Valerie giggled and leaned into his embrace. "I wasn't sure if she was exaggerating, so I looked it up when I got back to the room."

"Well, not right away." Terry laughed.

Val laughed.

Richard fought the urge to vomit.

"*Later*, I looked it up. It's true, and it's not just that people die. They die weirdly."

Stanley pushed the noodles about on his plate and mumbled.

Ed drained the amber liquid in his glass and burped. "What'd ya say? Didn't quite catch that."

Stanley jumped as if surprised to find there were other people sitting nearby. His gaze darted around the table. "I said, life is weird. Death is the only thing that's natural."

They all stared at him.

One corner of his mouth curled up. "Sorry. I suppose my thoughts have run toward the morbid lately."

Ed laughed. He raised his glass in the air and shook it. Luca bustled over with a fresh drink on a little brown tray.

Were they all going to ignore the obvious question? Richard asked Terry, "So, what makes their deaths weird?"

Terry poked his fork into his noodles and gave it a twist. "Every one of them was healthy when they boarded. They all died from heart attacks, and every one of them was found alone in bed with a big grin on their face."

Valarie shuddered. "Kitty—that's the hairdresser—Kitty said that the ship's doctor told her boyfriend, the ship's fitness director, that he'd never seen anything so creepy. They're just grinning with their eyes wide open like dying was the funniest thing that ever happened to them."

"The doctor is dating the fitness director?" Annie asked.

Valerie shook her head. "No. Kitty is dating the ship's fitness director."

"They're lesbians," Terry said, grinning.

"Might have to spend more time in the gym," Ed said.

Annie snorted. "You don't know what to do with one woman, let alone two."

A drop of sweat rolled down Richard's temple. He swiped it away. "How many?"

"Women?" Terry asked with a frown.

"Dead people!" The group at the next table over fell silent and gawked at Richard. He hadn't meant to shout. "How many have died?" he asked in a more reasonable tone.

"The one today makes twenty-three in six months," Valerie said.

Richard looked at Burke.

She gave a shake of her head, warning him not to talk about hunting in front of the others. "And they all died the same way?"

"Creepy, right?" Terry asked. He loosened his grip on Val long enough to lean forward and scoop some noodles into his mouth.

"This conversation is too macabre for my taste," Julia said. "Let us talk of life."

"I wanna hear more about the lesbians," Ed said.

Annie backhanded him on the shoulder.

"Excuse me," Burke murmured. She slid her chair back and glided away in a swirl of soft yellow cotton.

Richard watched her weave between the tables. She passed

the women's room and breezed out into the lobby. "Where's she going?" he asked Stanley.

Stanley looked up from his plate and studied the room with an expression like an elephant recently shot in the butt with a tranquilizer dart. He barely knew where he was, let alone where anyone else was going.

Without bothering to excuse himself, Richard tossed his napkin down next to his plate and chased the girl out of the dining room.

CHAPTER EIGHT

Burke

BURKE FLUNG HERSELF INTO A SQUASHY DECK CHAIR AND filled her lungs with the clean tropical air. Footsteps clattered across the wood and slowed as they approached. She looked up and saw her grandfather standing there. The man was a mess. One side of his shirt had come untucked. A drop of Alfredo sauce stained the lapel of his jacket. His hair stuck up every which way. She couldn't help the little laugh that escaped her lips.

"Why you laughing at me?" he demanded.

"I love you, Grandpa. I don't tell you that often enough."

He shuffled his feet. "I know it. Don't need the words."

"Words are nice to hear sometimes," she said.

"Yeah. Well..." He lowered himself into the chair next to her.

It was as close to *I love you too* as he was going to come, and she was okay with that. The very fact that he had agreed to come on the cruise with her was proof enough of his love. Words weren't his thing.

"You ran away pretty quick," he said.

She stared out at the rolling blue nothing. Who knew the ocean and Nebraska corn country had so much in common? The boat rocked from side to side with the gentle rhythm of a baby's cradle. "Did you see Stanley in there?"

Richard scowled. "I was sittin' right next to him."

She shook her head. "No, I mean did you *see* Stanley? He's so far inside his own head he barely knew what we were talking about. He doesn't ask questions anymore. He barely speaks, and when he does... Did you hear that thing he said about death?"

"We already knew Stan's in bad shape," Richard said.

Shoving down tears and guilt, she swallowed the hard-little lump in her throat. "This isn't working," she said. A gull fluttered overhead and landed somewhere above them. "He had the whole day to rest and he's worse than ever."

"Seems that way," Richard agreed.

"This thing with the people dying, it's probably not even our kind of thing. It's a run of bad luck for the cruise line, but kind of good luck for the passengers who are dying happy, right? I mean, there are worse ways to go than with a smile on your face."

"I reckon that's so," Richard said.

She growled at him, "Stop being so agreeable."

"You want me to argue?"

"It's what you do."

"I don't," he said and blew a raspberry at her.

She laughed, a short bark like a seal with a tobacco habit. "We're probably not going to find anything."

"No harm in looking." He stood up.

"What, now?"

"No time like the present. I got a badge in my pocket."

"Grandpa, you could have gotten in big trouble going through customs with fake ID!"

"The identity ain't fake, just the badge."

She rubbed her forehead with the tips of her fingers. "How are we even going to know where to look?"

He stuffed his hands in his pockets. "Stanley and I already been to the super suites once. Isn't that where the girl said the deaths happen? And besides, I walked all over this ship today and I know that whatever happened musta happened there, because nothing happened nowhere else."

Burke took a moment to follow that crazy train of logic and, strangely enough, couldn't find anything to argue about. "All right, we'll take a quick peek, but just a quick one, and then we'll head back up to the dining room in time to catch Stanley before he's done eating."

A LONG LINE OF FOLKS LEAVING THE DINING HALL WAITED IN front of the elevators.

"There must be stairs," Burke said.

They found a plain metal door around the corner from the elevators and descended past the first level. The second entryway they came to stood propped open. A red-faced kid of maybe twenty years, dressed in company blue and white, stood there with his hands held out in front of him in a "stop" gesture. His expression brought to mind a deer facing a Mack Truck. "Good evening, folks. May I ask which suite you're in?"

Richard glanced at Burke and she knew he was hoping

she'd do the talking. She told the kid the truth. "We're upstairs."

The guard nodded as if he'd suspected as much. "I apologize for any inconvenience, but this deck is off limits right now, except for those guests lodging here."

Richard tugged his fake FBI badge from his pocket and flashed it at the boy.

"We heard you had an unfortunate event today," Burke said. "We thought we'd check it out and offer to lend a hand. You don't mind, right?"

He blushed a shade deeper and glanced down the hall. "Well, uhm, it's nothing really out of the ordinary, really. On a ship of this size, sometimes there are things that happen."

A deep Southern voice echoed down the corridor, "Dammit! I said don't touch anything, and now you're telling me those idiots had their damn hands on every damn surface in this damn cabin?"

Burke raised an eyebrow at the kid who stared back.

His Adam's apple bobbed. "He'll be really mad if I let you through."

She smiled her widest, prettiest smile. "We're Feds. Everyone's really mad at us all the time. It's never stopped us before." She strolled past him, patting him on the shoulder as she went, and Richard hurried to keep up. They followed the ruckus to a door halfway down the hall, closed, but prevented from clicking tight by a deadbolt turned to the open position and propped against the latch plate. Burke hesitated. "Do not push this too far," she whispered.

He fiddled with his hearing aid. "Say again?"

She repeated herself.

He scowled at her. The hearing aid squealed. "What? Speak up!"

The door burst open. A slash-browed, thin-lipped man with fox-quick eyes stood there with his right hand on the handle. He was neither especially tall nor muscular, but Burke would have put good money on him in just about any fight. He bore within his aura the quality of a man who refused to be anything other than the most powerful person in the room—an alpha male, through and through.

"Is there something we can do to help you folks?" The words came straight out of the *How To Treat Guests* manual, but the tone was a strong shove against the wall that changed the question into something more akin to, "What do you think you're doing here, punk?"

Heat, not at all unpleasant, raced from Burke's belly into every part of her body. She tossed her head, making her earrings brush her shoulders. "Actually, we were hoping to help you."

Richard flashed his badge again. "FBI. We heard there was a death onboard."

"Not every death is a police matter. Certainly not a case for the FBI." The man stepped into the hallway and closed the door behind him, effectively blocking the view to the room. "Frankly, agents, we get a lot of elderly guests on our cruises. Death at sea is not as uncommon as some might think."

"Yet here you are, investigating," Burke pointed out. The clean, subtle scent of his cologne tickled her nose.

A muscle along his square jaw jumped. "Simply gathering personal effects and making sure we've taken care of every responsibility on our end."

"What's your name?" Richard asked.

The man dragged his gaze from Burke's eyes to Richard's. "Gordon Westchester. I'm head of ship security."

"Richard Bell." Richard held out a hand and let it hang in

mid-air for several seconds before slipping it into his pocket. "This is my associate, Burke Martin. I gotta be honest, Gordon." He gestured to their opulent surroundings. "All this luxury and comfort, it's not what I'm used to. I dragged my partner down here because I'm too danged cozy. It don't feel natural to relax this much. We'd be genuinely happy to lend a hand in any way we can."

The man twitched as if he were shaking off an irritating fly. "Forgive my saying so, but you seem a bit past retirement age."

"I guess they value the wisdom of my years."

"Yeah. 'Cause that's how it works." He focused on Burke again and his voice rolled over her like a stiff drink, "I'm sorry, but a passenger death is not a form of entertainment for our more intrepid guests. If you're looking for something a little wild, might I suggest the waterslide? I hear it's fantastic."

Burke lifted her chin an inch. "Mr. Westchester, I think you underestimate our abilities."

His flashing eyes shifted back to her. "I wouldn't dare underestimate an esteemed agent of the United States Government, Agent Martin, but this is not your jurisdiction. Even if it were, like I said, there's nothing to investigate. Good evening."

With that, the man returned to the room from which he'd come and closed the door, this time engaging the deadbolt rather than using it as a prop.

Richard harrumphed. "He doesn't seem to want our help."

Burke raised one brow. "Ya think?"

"Seems a bit hostile."

"A bit," she agreed.

"How's that make you feel?" he asked.

"Since when do you ask people about their feelings?" She retraced their path toward the kid at the staircase.

"Well, you're all pink-cheeked and sweaty. Thought maybe you were gonna pop him in the kisser or something."

Or something. That voice. The man could take up a second career reading sexy romance novels to lonely middle-aged women. Not that she counted herself as lonely or middle-aged. She reached up and wiped her brow. "I don't know what you're talking about." At the end of the hall, she smiled at the guard again. "Your boss is a friendly fellow."

The guy laughed. "Yeah. Very. You should see him at the company Christmas party."

"I bet. Good luck to you," she said.

"Enjoy the cruise, agents," he replied.

Richard huffed and puffed along behind her up two flights of stairs. "Hey," he said, just as they reached the dining room deck.

She glanced over her shoulder.

"That line's probably gone by now. We could have taken the elevator."

"That's true, but the stairs are better for you," she told him.

"The stairs are better for you," he shot back in a mocking, high-pitched voice. "Dang kid. You're trying to health me into the grave."

"Yes. You caught me." She imagined she could feel her grandfather making faces at her back.

They returned to the dining room to find the seats all but empty and the cleaning staff getting the room ready for the midnight buffet. Dishes clinked. A vacuum sweeper ran in a far corner. The lingering aroma of garlic hung in the air like the ghost of the meal now gone, but Stanley was nowhere to be seen.

"Crap. He's gone."

Richard caught up and looked around. "Probably went to bed."

She threw up her hands. "That's what I was trying to prevent. I thought you wanted to get him active. I thought that's what this whole witch hunt boiled down to for you."

That perked him up. "Ha! So, you agree it sounds witchy."

She sighed. "I don't know, but we're on vacation. They're saying it was natural causes. Maybe we should accept it as natural causes for now."

He tugged her arm to turn her toward him. "I need you to believe me. I know in my bones there is something more going on around here than anyone is copping to."

Her shoulders sagged. She covered his hand with hers. "I do believe you, Grandpa. I just don't know if it's right to drag Stanley into it. I don't know if it's right to leave him out. I have no idea which end is up anymore." All those words flew out of her mouth before she thought to hold them captive inside her, but now that they were free, some thick rusty chain inside her broke apart and crumbled to dust.

Richard nodded. "I weren't never this frustrated at the old folk's home."

"Really?"

"Nah. That's a lie." He blew out a sigh that made his lips flap like a tired old horse's. "Now, what do we do?"

No way was she going to let Stanley lay around in bed waiting for death. "Well, Stanley doesn't want to be active, but he's always been a night owl. If we can't get him in motion, maybe we can at least entertain him."

CHAPTER NINE

Gordon

TWO MEN HOISTED THE BEEFY DEAD GUY OFF THE BED. THE one at the head lost his grip and the corpse hit the floor with a hard thump that sent a shudder through the entire group. Gordon chomped down on his third antacid in less than an hour. He needed real cops, not kids fresh out of college who'd never done more than write a parking citation. The handlers finally managed to get the body situated in the bag and close the zipper. Gordon turned his attention to the other guy—the one with the weird Nordic name.

"What was it you were trying to tell me?"

The kid's Adam's apple bobbed up and down. "Well, it's just that we thought you wanted us to look for clues, so we opened drawers and such and..." He chewed on his lip rather than finish the sentence.

"Son, you need to finish that sentence before I throw your skinny ass overboard just to hear the splash."

He whined now, "We didn't realize you were planning on asking for fingerprints."

Gordon might have been able to deal with the incompetence, but incompetence compounded by whining was more than he could handle. The tenuous grip he held on his temper slipped. "Dammit! I said don't touch anything and now you're telling me those idiots have had their damn hands on every damn surface in this damn cabin?"

"Not every surface, no sir. I don't think so."

Gordon rubbed his temples and tried to lower his blood pressure before he suffered a stroke or something. Keep it together. The crime scene wasn't necessarily a total waste. Besides, the fingerprint thing was a long shot, and it would mean involving the police when they got to shore, assuming they'd even believe there was a case. And if they did believe this was a case, the press would be all over it. He'd never cover up a crime, but neither did he feel it was in anyone's best interest to turn every bad thing that happened in the world into post-dinner entertainment for the masses.

"Say again!"

He looked around for the source of the voice. It came from just outside the door. Who the hell would be down here at this hour? Most passengers would be enjoying their too-rich dinner or settling in to watch the night's entertainment.

"What? Speak up!"

He stormed across the room and yanked open the door. An old guy an inch or two shorter than him with wild white hair and a stain on his jacket stood next to a tall, muscular woman with a wide mouth and upturned eyes that were, at the moment, wide and startled. She didn't flinch from him. She braced for attack. The shift in her posture was subtle but unmistakable. Cop or military. He wasn't sure which, but he'd bet his life on one or the other. Either way, she had no business there and he intended to get rid of her and the old fart as fast as possible. "Is there something we can do to help you folks?"

The woman squared her shoulders. "Actually, we were hoping to help you."

The old guy withdrew a badge that he showed too quickly for Gordon to read, but the three bold black letters in the center were plain enough. "FBI. We heard there was a death onboard."

Of course, they'd heard. The little Brazilian brat probably told his girlfriend the hairdresser. Half the damn ship was no doubt talking about the death. Was it too much to ask for a staff who could obey a single damn order? He shoved all that to the back of his mind and focused on the fire burning in front of him. "Not every death is a police matter. Certainly not a case for the FBI." He realized they could probably see the three officers in the room rifling through drawers and luggage, and stepped into the hallway so he could close the door. "Frankly, agents, we get a lot of elderly guests on our cruises. Death at sea is not as uncommon as some might think."

"Yet here you are, investigating," the woman said.

Gordon narrowed his eyes on her and wished he had someone half as sharp helping him figure out what the hell was going on. "Simply gathering personal effects and making sure we've taken care of every responsibility on our end."

"What's your name?" the man asked.

Maybe he should tell them. Maybe he could let this striking woman carry some of the weighty burden he'd been crushed under these past several weeks. Then again, maybe Neptune himself would rise out of the water and hand him a few answers. He focused on the man. "Gordon Westchester. I'm head of ship security."

"Richard Bell." He held out a hand, which Gordon refused to shake. He wasn't going to be won over by a career Fed who'd read *How To Win Friends and Influence People* back in the 1980s. After a moment, the guy slipped his hand into his pocket and tried hard not to look peeved at the rejection. "This is my associate, Burke Martin." He went on with a bunch of yadda yadda yadda that boiled down to exactly what Gordon had been trying to avoid. They were bored and looking for excitement.

Was he being punished? Did he have some sort of bad karma? Take a job on a cruise ship, they said. It'll be like drawing an extra check for living it up with the rest of the retired folks, they said. He'd had less stress worrying about IEDs detonating under his Jeep than he did on this cursed boat.

With monumental effort, he managed not to yell. Instead, he calmly and reasonably explained that dead passengers were not part of the provided entertainment.

Agent Martin lifted her chin. "Mr. Westchester, I think you underestimate our abilities."

Oh, how wrong she was. He knew exactly what she was capable of. What she found, and what she'd be required by law and ethics to do with that information once she found it, could very well shut down not just the *Diversion*, but the entire cruise line. He needed to get rid of her. He'd figure out what was killing the passengers and put a stop to the deaths, without destroying his livelihood and that of thousands of other people.

He'd rooted terrorists out of the caves they'd holed up in. He could root this killer out of whatever foxhole he'd curled up in and he didn't need some other cop to do it, no matter how easy on the eyes she might be.

Before the tiny voice in the back of his mind that whispered about pride and hard falls could cause him any hesitation, he dismissed the two interlopers and returned to the room, carefully locking the door behind him.

The Nordic kid held up a tiny plastic sword like an offering to an angry god. "We found this."

"What is it?" Gordon asked.

"They use them in the bar, you know, like to put a cherry in a drink or something."

Gordon rolled his eyes. "Well, thanks be. The mystery's solved." He gestured to the body. "Get him up to the morgue and, for the love of Pete, try to be discreet." He pointed at the other security guard, the one who'd cowered in the corner for the past several minutes. "You, pack up the man's effects. Log everything. Even the damn toothpick. So help me, if I find one thing that's not on that ledger when you're done—"

"Sir, you can count on me to do it right, Sir," the guy squeaked.

Gordon reached for another antacid, but he'd already emptied the roll.

CHAPTER TEN

Richard

ROUSING STANLEY INTO ACTION TOOK SO LONG THAT THE show had already started when they arrived. Music spilled into the foyer outside the lounge. The song stirred a vague memory of standing on the factory line, the odor of hot plastic singing his nose hairs. The guys at Wellington Plastics must have listened to the same song while they worked. They always had some modern crap playing on the radio.

"What's the face? You don't like Prince?" Burke grinned at him.

"Prince who?" Richard asked.

"Actually, I believe it's the Artist Formerly Known as Prince," Stanley said.

Richard harrumphed. "Oh, *now* you've got something to say."

Stanley shrugged. "There is great power in names."

"Oh, no." Burke lurched to a dead stop just inside the open

double doors. Richard and Stanley drew up on either side of her.

"Who crapped in your cornflakes?" Richard asked.

"What?" she snapped. "No one. I'm just not sure about staying."

Richard scanned the dark room. Most of the light came from little white candles floating in vases full of colorful glass beads and water, and lamps pointed at the geometric shapes that passed for art on the walls. In contrast, the stage dazzled the eyes with flashing rainbow lights. A tiny man with impressively tall hair pranced in high-heeled shoes and a stretchy purple bodysuit.

"I met him earlier," Burke said.

"The singer?"

She nodded. "He was way too flirty. Creepy flirty, you know?"

"He's human," Stanley said. "He sings as if he's a man who understands mortality."

Richard couldn't deny it. The man had a voice like an angel. Too bad he wasted it on nonsense songs about purple rain.

"I never thought he was a monster. I think he's a creepy guy. I've had my fill of horrible human men lately, in case you've forgotten."

Stanley blanched like she'd slapped him.

Burke immediately back peddled. "I'm making too much of it. I'm sure he was just being friendly. Let's sit over there." She marched off toward a table near the right side of the stage, apparently assuming the men would follow. Of course, they did.

The singer finished his song and wiped his face with a fluffy pink towel. His gaze passed over the crowd and snapped back to Burke. "This next song is dedicated to a smart and very beautiful lady. Perhaps next time we meet, we won't be interrupted." He winked and launched into his song, "You don't have to be beautiful to turn me on."

"I'm leaving." She started to rise, but Richard caught her wrist.

"Oh no you don't, little girl. You're the one who brought us here. Now we're going to stay."

She looked at Stanley. "You should tell him to let me go."

Stanley folded his hands on the table. "I was perfectly content to settle in with a cup of tea. They were showing "Casablanca" on channel sixty-four."

Burke rolled her eyes and flopped back in her chair.

The guy on the stage dropped to his knees, held his arms out to her, and sang his heart out.

Burke dropped her face into her hand.

A waitress in a skirt so short Richard could see the edges of the moonrise, approached their table. "Can I bring you a drink?"

"God, yes," Burke said. "A dirty vodka martini, please."

"You got coffee? Fully leaded?" Richard asked.

"Sure," the waitress said.

"Coffee? At this hour?" Burke asked.

Richard scowled at her. "You ain't my wife or my doctor, are you?"

She crossed her arms and turned toward the stage. The singer made kissing noises at her.

Richard laughed under his breath. He looked at Stanley to enjoy the joke with him, but Stanley may as well have been a bump on a log for all the emotion he displayed. Richard slumped in his chair. A cup of coffee was placed in front of him. He slurped it up and watched the other folks in the room. Most that he could see were watching the singer with wide eyes and little smiles. Apparently, people enjoyed this kind of music. Richard was bored. He poked Burke. "So, tell me who this clown is."

She sighed. "I was at the pool today, trying to mind my own business and read a book. He showed up, basically naked, and started hitting on me. Then Greg called—"

Richard almost choked on his coffee. "Greg called? What does he need from you?"

The corners of her eyes crinkled. "He said he has a feeling something bad is going to happen."

"Something bad is going to happen if he keeps bothering you." He slurped his coffee. "I thought he was in a Mosque in Colorado."

She played with the little plastic sword in her drink. "He left. He's on his way to Santa Fe to hook up with some kind of spiritual community there."

Richard looked at Stanley. Stanley stared at the stage, showing as much interest as a stalk of broccoli. He gave him a light slap on the shoulder. Stanley jumped like a bomb went off.

"Calm yourself down, old man. I was just going to ask you what you think about ol' Greg moving to Santa Fe."

Stanley blinked. "Greg?"

"My ex-husband," Burke said.

"I thought he was in a monastery in Colorado."

"Someone is in a monastery? What a waste of a man." Julia had come up behind Richard, stealthy as a tiger.

Richard banged his coffee cup down on the table. "Woman! It ain't right to sneak up on a man like that!"

She waved away his words. The flashing stage lights refracted from her jewels. "May I join you? I think Isaac makes a wonderful Prince." She pulled out a chair and sat without waiting for an answer.

"Prince Isaac?" Richard couldn't remember ever hearing of the man.

Julie laughed. "You are a card, Richard."

Burke laid a hand on his arm. "Prince is the artist who originally created this music. Isaac is a Prince impersonator."

Richard finished off his coffee. "Well great. Thanks for coming over to our table, Ms. Domina, but we were just leaving." He pushed his chair back.

Burke's grip tightened on his arm. "Oh no, Grandpa. You insisted we stay. We're going to stay."

Julia grinned.

Richard picked up his cup, found it empty, and plunked it back down on the table. From the corner of his eye, he caught a glimpse of the activities director weaving among the passengers. He figured if he was stuck, they were all going to be stuck. He waved his arms in the air until the big galoot noticed him.

A slow smile spread across Ike's face.

Richard watched as Ike excused himself from the other table and homed in on Stanley.

"Good evening," he said, spreading his gorilla arms wide. "I'm delighted to see you all enjoying our program. Stanley— you didn't tell me the reason you nap all day is because you love the nightlife."

Stanley's face twitched. Was that an attempt at a smile? Richard scowled.

"Tomorrow is a big day, right? First landfall." He pointed a sausage-like finger in Stanley's direction. "I absolutely insist on you going ashore. You must visit the old Fort San Cristobal." His eyes narrowed and he cocked his head as if to study

Stanley more closely. "I have a feeling you enjoy a little adventure more than you let on."

Stanley's eyes took on the weird far-away glaze that was fast becoming all too familiar. "I did."

Julia leaned in close to Richard. "What about you?" If she was a cat, she'd be purring in his ear. "Do you like adventure? Are you going to tour the fort?" Her hand landed softly on his knee.

He squeaked like a church mouse.

"Just think of all those men, tied up in chains in that dungeon."

Ike whistled. "There's a thought for you. I've got to say, though, the whole pirate thing has never been my bag. I'm a bigger fan of the James Bond type. Give me a man with a titanium spine and a powerful mind and I'll be in love forever."

Richard ignored him. He'd forgotten about the old fort and its famous dungeon. He knew, if he was a monster, that's the kind of place where he'd want to live.

At last, the show ended and the three of them managed to escape the clutches of their admirers.

After Richard changed into his PJs and brushed his teeth, he settled into bed with the guest information binder from the nightstand drawer. As he'd hoped, several pages were dedicated to the city of San Juan and its famous landmark. Fueled by caffeine and rising panic over Stanley's meek condition, he set to learning as much as possible before they dropped anchor.

CHAPTER ELEVEN

Richard

THE TOURISTS DISEMBARKED BEFORE THE ANCIENT CITADEL and stood in a cluster gaping at the towering structure before them. Mother nature had worked her creative magic on the bricks, chipping away at them with relentless wind and then filling the cracks with bright green moss. A little thrill tripped through Richard's innards. If they'd pulled up in front of an abandoned insane asylum built atop an ancient Indian burial ground, they'd have less chance of finding monsters than they did in this place. This was the kind of place that spawned every good ghost story ever told. He broke away from the pack and headed toward the entrance.

"Grandpa!"

He looked over his shoulder.

Burke nodded toward Stanley. The old peacock's new standard pace was half a degree faster than molasses in January.

Richard huffed and waited for the two of them to catch up while most of the folks from the cruise ship passed in front of them. The Cadwalladers moseyed along at the rear of the pack, slower even than Stanley, holding hands and giggling over their whispered nonsense.

"Let them go on ahead, Grandpa. It might be best if we have a little space, right?" Burke nodded in Stanley's direction.

Richard scratched his head and then tried to settle his hair. Maybe he should cut it all off. He'd match Burke and Stanley.

The little group tottered beneath an arched opening into a long hallway. Obviously, someone this side of the twentieth century had whitewashed the walls and ceiling. Not too far on this side, though, judging by the cracks and missing chunks of plaster.

At the end of the bright corridor, a set of iron bars with a gate in the center had been set into the brick. The gate stood propped open for all the merry tourists who wished to enter with their bright smiles and flashing cell phone cameras. Once past that gate, the hallway resembled an old Tombstone mine-shaft except for the occasional tiny rectangle that had been built into the wall to let in a bit of light. Passing through those sunbeams caused their shadows to leap and dance along the curved wall. Richard thought about shadow demons and shivered. He peeked over at Burke. Her spine resembled a piece of rebar. "You all right?"

"Great, thanks."

Stanley, the good pet, kept pace at her side.

"This is so creepy," Valerie said. "Can't you imagine some poor prisoner being marched down this hallway, knowing he'd never walk free again?"

"They were pirates, Val. Not exactly innocent young men," Terry said.

Richard had lived long enough to know that not every pirate was a bad guy and not every man in prison deserved to be there, but he lacked the energy to engage in a philosophical debate with the giggly children. He pulled the EMF detector from his pocket. The blinking lights flashed past green and yellow, straight to bright red. A gentle elbow in the ribs got Burke's attention and she looked at the gauge.

"I don't see anything though," she said.

Richard's skin crawled. He hated to agree with the vapid Valerie, but she was right. You could practically hear the echoing footsteps of doomed men being dragged in chains through the dank tunnel. EMF said their spirits lingered, trapped here by the trauma of their deaths, but none of them seemed to possess the strength to actually manifest as anything more than a cool breeze. They couldn't hunt a ghost who couldn't make itself visible.

They ducked through another low iron gate into a space so dark that some of the tourists turned on their phones' flashlights to get a better look. Words, and images of ships and men, had been scrawled onto the plaster walls. Tiny dark cells with stone floors held nothing corporeal, though the EMF's digital readout had gone off the charts.

"Their energy has saturated the walls," Stanley said, running his hand over a gruesome-looking red smear near one of the door frames. "There is no spirit haunting this place, Richard. This place *is* a haunt. The very walls are held together by death and pain. Trying to isolate a single ghost would be like trying to extract a fossil from rock."

The three of them stepped into the hallway and found themselves alone. "Where are Terry and Val?" Burke asked.

Richard blew a raspberry. "Probably communing with dolphins or something. Come on."

They retraced their steps, merging into a flowing river of

tourists heading back out into the tropical sun. Outside, Richard blinked against the aggressive light.

"Why don't you wear your sunglasses?" Burke asked.

"I left them in the room."

"I bought them for you to protect your eyes, you know."

"Lived more than eighty years without protecting them. Don't figure this will be the day they fail."

She rolled her eyes and turned away. "What's that?"

Richard looked where she pointed. Half a dozen black and white police cruises clustered like enormous insects near the side of the old fort. A growing crowd of tourists choked the area. Why spend time studying ancient misery when fresh misery lay at hand?

Two old women rolled in their direction on bright red electric scooters.

Burke stepped into their path. "Excuse me. Do you know what happened?"

"Some local boys found a body," one of the women said. She shook her head. "Terrible. Just terrible. Such tragedy in such a beautiful place."

"It was a murder," the other woman said.

"You don't know that, Helen," the first one replied.

"Well, why else would there be half a dozen police cars?" Helen asked.

"I didn't see any blood."

"You can kill a man without making him bloody. Haven't you ever watched those CSI shows?"

"I don't watch television, Helen. It rots the mind."

"Your mind is rotten."

"Better my mind than my woman parts."

Burke turned away, her eyebrows high. "Okay. Thanks for

the info." She made shooing gestures at Richard and Stanley and Richard happily moved along.

They found Terry and Valerie at the edge of the crowd of gawkers. Val saw them coming. Her hair hung half out of the elastic band that held it back. Damp curls stuck to her face and neck. She brushed one away. "I can't believe some kid found him that way."

Richard stood on tiptoes to see past all the other rubber-neckers. A white sheet had been spread over something, presumably the body. "What happened?"

"Kid started screaming. Next thing I saw, there were cops everywhere," Terry said. He shifted and Richard noticed three parallel gashes on the left side of his face.

"What the devil happened to you?"

Terry's gaze darted to Val. Her cheeks blushed a pretty pink.

Richard held up his hand. "Nevermind. I don't want to know." He wished he'd thought to bring his badge. Maybe they'd have let him ask a few questions. Then again, he wasn't sure the FBI would have any clout in Puerto Rico. He never had been able to quite work out whether or not the island was part of the USA.

Just then, he heard Burke call out, "Stanley, wait up!"

She was running off after Stan, who was halfway back to the parking lot. Richard plodded along in her wake.

Stanley turned and waited, adjusting his little gray newsboy cap to block the sun from his eyes. "I'm very tired. I'd like to return to the ship now."

Richard noted the dark circles under Stanley's eyes and the way his arm trembled, even as he clutched the silver head of his cane.

"You sick?" Richard asked.

Stanley's sad little smile appeared. "Not in body, my friend."

Richard glanced back at the commotion by the fortress.

"Go," Burke told him. "I'll make sure Stanley gets to his room safely."

He hadn't realized how deeply he wanted to find out what had happened until she freed him to investigate.

Just as he arrived, the coroner enlisted one of the uniformed cops to help him lift the body onto a gurney. Richard barged past the other gawkers. "Excuse me?"

Both men looked at him.

"I'm with the FBI out of Michigan. What happened here?"

"Nothing that concerns the American federal government, I assure you," the coroner said.

"If someone's been murdered—"

"There was no murder here, agent. This man collapsed on the rocks. There are no signs of foul play. In fact, he died with a smile on his face. Now, if you'll excuse us, we need to inform his family what happened."

Richard backed away to let the men work. His mind told him that the officials were likely right. The man just died. His churning gut demanded a better explanation. The details remained fuzzy, but the punchline was as clear as the tropical sky. The *Diversion* harbored a monster.

RICHARD SHUFFLED ALONGSIDE THE BREAKFAST BUFFET WITH all the other happy campers. Burke craned her neck to see what he was scooping into his bowl. "You're eating oatmeal and fruit?"

"You judging?"

She sprinkled a spoonful of granola over her yogurt. "I wouldn't dare. It's not my place to comment on how you must be suffering from all the crap you've eaten in the past three days."

"Smart aleck kid," he grumbled as he stalked toward an empty table.

Once Burke and Stanley had taken their seats and the omnipresent Luca had fetched their juice and coffee, Richard pointed his spoon in Stanley's direction. "I'd think a man would need more than toast and jam after skipping supper. You musta had a great sleep, though. What was it? Thirteen hours?"

"You judging?" he asked.

Burke snickered.

Richard tossed her an evil glare. "Anyway, I ask because the itinerary in that folder in my room says there are some pretty high-class stores at this stop. Seemed right up your alley."

Stanley gave a tiny shake of his head. "Thank you, but I believe I'll stay on the ship. Yesterday was difficult. I'll just rest for now."

"Did I hear someone say they're in need of rest?" Ike bounced up to their table like a rock-solid, three-hundred-pound chocolate Labrador. "I could recommend the nine a.m. yoga class or a vitamin smoothie from our fantastic juice bar." His eyes locked on Stanley's. "Or perhaps you'd enjoy a full-body deep tissue massage?"

Stanley sipped his tea. "I'm quite certain a good old-fashioned nap will suffice."

Ike pressed an enormous hand against the brick wall of his chest. "I can't bear it. Stanley, if I didn't know better, I'd say you aren't enjoying yourself. I'm a failure if I can't find some fabulous way for you to while away the hours. Perhaps a few hours in the casino?"

Stanley shook his head. "I've had a run of bad luck lately. I'm not sure a casino is a good idea."

"Perhaps shuffleboard?"

"Stan ain't a big drinker," Richard said.

"Then you must spend some time lounging poolside," Ike said.

"I don't—" Stanley began, but Ike cut him off.

"I simply won't take no for an answer. I insist. I'm going to come and check up on you, and if you're not having fun by the pool, I may be forced to take drastic measures." He gave Burke a little wink. "I'm counting on your help, here."

"You've got it," she assured him. "Since the moment we parked the car in Miami, I've been telling Stanley he needs to relax and have fun."

Ike slapped Richard on the back. "Fantastic. I'll see you all by the pool after breakfast.

RICHARD STARED AT THE RIDICULOUS OLD MAN IN THE mirror. Maybe Captain Roy and Stan's boyfriend, Gigantor, turned a healthy shade of bronze under the sun, but his own papery old hide glowed a sickly, burnt pinkish brown. In contrast, his hair appeared brighter white than ever. It floated around his head in pathetic wisps he couldn't even think of as clouds. More like the contrails drawn across the sky by passing jets. The sunglasses Burke pressed him to wear were in no danger of falling off, balanced as they were upon his elephantine nose and ears. A white tee shirt did nothing to hide his sunken chest or swollen gut, but it did manage to highlight the absurdly bright colors of his brand new swim trunks. Yellow and orange. What in the name of all that was holy possessed the girl to buy him yellow and orange trunks? At least his black socks and sensible white sneakers suited him. From toes to mid-shin, he was properly dressed.

"Good Lord," he muttered, and he swore an oath to his mirror image that if anyone other than his own people were at the pool, he'd turn straight around, put on some real clothes, and spend the rest of the afternoon watching television.

He waited for Burke's knock on the door and opened it to find her dressed like a tropical dream in a white bikini top and some kind of half-transparent skirt that hung from her hips. Stanley stood next to her in navy blue trunks and a white shirt.

"Really?" Richard threw up his hands. "You got him navy blue and you bought this for me?"

She cocked her head to one side. "Stanley went to the store himself and picked out his own clothes. As I recall, you muttered something along the lines of, 'This trip was your idea. Just get me whatever you think is right, 'cause I ain't spending a whole day shopping at Walmart.'"

Richard pushed past her and peeked in both directions. The coast was clear.

Luck stayed with him all the way to the elevator and onto the ship's deck. A few folks lay about in the sun, greased up like so many chicken breasts in a fryer. He carefully avoided eye contact and made it all the way to the bubbling hot tub next to the pool. Blessings from Heaven! Not another soul to be found.

He perched on the edge of a lawn chair to untie and remove his sneakers and socks. He tucked the latter inside the former and planted his feet wide on the hot boards of the deck. No-slip strips made of something resembling course-grade sandpaper scratched his soles. Both hips and both knees snapped like dry sticks when he pushed up from the too-low chair. He edged over to the side of the water and dipped a foot in.

Hot!

His nose twitched with the smell of bleach.

Burke and Stanley were talking to each other. He couldn't hear them over the racket of the jacuzzi jets, but Stanley didn't look happy. Of course, that was nothing new. Guy resembled Droopy dog every day. The two of them settled into lounge chairs.

Fine with Richard. Let the rest of them fry under the sun. He intended to boil himself in this chemical soup and enjoy every last minute of it.

Clutching the silver rail, he maneuvered down four steps and sank onto his butt on the concrete bench. The steaming water bubbled all the way up to his shoulders. His muscles melted like butter in a cast-iron skillet. With his head resting against the edge of the tub and his eyes closed against the sun's assault, his mind began chewing on the events of the past few days.

He mentally retraced every step. First, they boarded. Nothing weird there unless you count Julia standing in the shadows making eyes at innocent travelers. There was the stupid safety spiel with the lovely French girl, Nikki. Dinner was strange, but not in a supernatural sort of way. The skinny waiter, Terry and Val, Ed and Annie, and Julia struck him as weirdos, but they all walked in the sun and ate mashed potatoes and seemed human enough. 'Course, witches were human, more or less.

Some tiny synapse in the farthest back corner of his mind threw up a flare of an idea in the dark sky of his thoughts. He'd seen something at dinner that night that did strike him as odd, but he couldn't quite remember what it was. He tried to catch the thought, but it fluttered around his mind like a humming-bird on crack. Better to move on. Maybe it would come to him if he didn't focus too hard on it.

On their first full day aboard the ship, they'd seen the two women arguing in the hall. The girl Isabelle compared the ship to a live-action version of a TV crime drama, but that could be explained by what they learned from Valerie about the deaths aboard the *Diversion*. Then again, the natural death of an old fogey was hardly the makings of TV crime drama. The ghost hunt turned up bupkis and just about did ol' Stanley in, even though the ship was as empty of spirits as an exorcist training camp. Lunch with Ed and Annie turned up the tidbit about that crazy old bat, Julia.

His thoughts began to drift apart like wisps of clouds painted across the clear blue sky. Probably, it would be a bad idea to fall asleep in the hot tub. He could slip under, or drown, or have a heat stroke and end up back in Everest or someplace similar, wishing he'd drowned. He forced his eyes open and sat up.

Julia grinned at him.

"Argh!"

"Hello, Darling. You seemed to be on the other side of the universe. I was starting to wonder if I should be worried." She sat perched on the edge of the tub with her feet in the water, an exotic bird with a distinctly predatory aura. The emeralds on her fingers and ears matched the deep greens in the peacock pattern of her swimsuit with its tiny skirt that did nothing to hide the shapely curve of her thigh. She stepped into the water and cozied in next to Richard.

He jumped up and searched for Burke and Stanley. They

were gone. Vanished. Left him there to fend for himself with this she-wolf. Ungrateful, unloyal, thoughtless couple of...

"Richard? You are all right, aren't you?"

Her fingers brushed his leg, just north of the knee.

Richard stumbled away from her tentacles. "I'm fine. I was fine. Now my whole train of thought derailed. That's what I get for wanting to relax in peace for a few minutes."

"Peace is overrated, Richard. Seek excitement." Her foot hooked his ankle.

Richard was all the way back to his room when he realized that he'd run away so fast, he'd left his socks and shoes by the pool.

He could call Burke and ask her to pick them up.

He thought about trying to explain.

Forget it. He'd find some new shoes in one of the little shops. And if he couldn't find any, so be it. He'd go to dinner barefoot before he went up to the pool again.

CHAPTER TWELVE

Richard

BURKE TOSSED THE MAKE-UP BRUSH ONTO THE MINISCULE bathroom vanity. The air had grown steadily hotter and more humid as they sailed. At this point, make-up seemed like a waste of time.

Isn't that what you came on this trip for? To waste time?

"I came on this trip to help Stanley," she told her reflection. Then she became annoyed. "You spend too much time talking to yourself."

She left the bathroom before she managed to work herself up into a full-blown argument. She retrieved the pink maxi-dress she'd chosen for dinner from its hanger, let it slide over her body, then slipped her feet into her favorite white sandals.

After a few fortifying breaths, she exited her little room and banged on her grandfather's door.

"I'm comin'. Don't need to bust it down," he shouted.

She rolled her eyes.

A moment later, he yanked the door open and glared at her. "What do you want?"

"It's time to go to dinner. What are you so mad about?"

"I ain't mad." Richard returned to his room and sat down on the bed to put on his shoes. He left the door open.

She noted the unfamiliar black and gray sneakers. "Did you go shopping?"

He made a noise like an old diesel truck running out of fuel.

"What?"

"You left me."

"What?" she asked again.

"You up and left. Stan, too, without so much as a by your leave."

"I told you I was taking Stanley to get a hat. His head was burning up. When we came back, you were gone. I figured you'd be back for your shoes, but you never came."

Richard let his foot fall to the floor. "You never told me nothin'."

"I did."

"You didn't."

She threw up her hands.

"You think I'm crazy?" he asked.

"Not crazy, but maybe deaf."

"Smart aleck kid!"

"Stubborn old man!"

They glared at each other while the low rumble of the engines and the sloshing of water filled the dead air between them.

"You coming to dinner?" she asked.

"Don't enjoy sharing my meals with a bunch of freaks."

If rolling her eyes burned calories, she'd waste away to nothing.

"Are you coming?"

"Yeah, yeah. I'm coming."

They collected Stanley and she prompted the two men toward the dining room like a mother hen urging her chicks to the feeding tray.

"Where's the rest of them?" her grandfather asked upon catching sight of their table, where Ed and Annie sat alone.

Burke ignored him. How was she supposed to know?

By the time they'd taken their seats, Annie resembled a tick about to pop. "Did you hear?"

"Apparently, I'm a deaf old man who can't hear nothin'," Richard said.

Ed chuckled.

Burke caught Luca's attention and asked for a glass of cabernet. He dashed away as if he'd been sent on a quest for the Holy Grail.

"Another death," Annie blurted out the moment Luca stepped out of earshot.

Burke's heart skipped a beat. "What happened?"

"It's the same as the others. They're saying natural causes, but Captain Northrup looked very concerned when we saw him." She nudged Ed with her elbow. "Didn't you think he looked upset?"

"Looked like crap on a cracker," Ed said.

Burked searched the room. Captain Northrup sat at his designated table with four couples. They were laughing about something, but even at a distance, she could tell his laugh was strained. He sat with his spine curved as if bowed by life's pressures.

"Who told you this?" Richard asked.

"I went to Val's girl in the salon. Didn't she do a wonderful job?" She patted the snowdrift on top of her head. "That girl never seems to leave the salon, but she knows everything about everything that happens on this ship. Do you know what she told me?" She glanced around and then leaned forward. "That hunky activities director is a homosexual."

Ed choked on his cocktail.

Burke folded her hands in her lap. She breathed deeply and intentionally until the adrenaline pounding through her system settled down. "What did she tell you about the death?"

Annie happily left the topic of Ike's sexuality to relate the gruesome details she'd picked up, "The man was traveling alone, and he was a regular King Midas. When they found him, he was fully clothed, flat on his back on a rumpled bed, grinning ear-to-ear."

Luca bustled up with a tray full of rectangular saucers, each bearing one half of an egg approximately the same size as a quarter. "Compliments of the chef."

Richard scowled at his plate. "What in the name of Sam Hill is this supposed to be?"

Luca wrapped his long arms around himself as if trying to hold in his joy. "Tonight's amuse-bouche is a stuffed quail egg with horse radish garnish."

"You yanking my chain?" Richard asked.

The server's gaze darted to Burke.

"Don't mind him," she said. "He's an old curmudgeon."

Luca gave a wavy grin and nodded. "Enjoy."

Burke popped the egg in her mouth.

"Stanley, what do you make of this?" she asked.

Stanley shrugged one bony shoulder. "It's not really any concern of ours."

She wanted to scream, to shake him, to slap his face and

demand he snap out of it. Instead, she twisted the linen napkin lying across her thighs.

The next two courses passed in a blur of Annie's chatter. As Luca presented their burgundy braised short ribs, Julia swooped into the room in a swirl of creamy silk and onyx. The color suited her. She looked ten years younger than she had the night she'd dressed in red.

Luca held her chair for her. "Shall I start your meal with the salad, Ms. Domina?"

She beamed up at him. "You're a darling, but I've already eaten. I just came for the company. Perhaps a cocktail, though?"

"As you wish. The usual?"

"Please."

He sliced through the dining room to fetch her drink.

"What have I missed?" she asked.

Ed answered, heedless of the sauce on his chin, "My woman's gossiping. Dick don't approve of teensy-weensy deviled eggs, and the newlyweds couldn't drag themselves out of bed to join us for dinner."

"If they're in bed, it's because they're recuperating," Julia said, folding her hands like a steeple.

"Recuperating?" Burke asked.

Julia nodded. "I saw them, not an hour ago, coming off the elevator. She had terrible dark circles." She pointed to the area beneath her eye. The flesh there lay beneath so thick a layer of make-up, it might have been applied with a putty knife. "The boy had a real shiner and scratch on his cheek and arm."

"What do you think happened?" Annie asked.

Ed chuckled. "Sounds about right for a honeymoon."

"Stanley, how's your food?" Burke asked, desperate to redirect the conversation before it completely derailed.

Stanley looked at the plate in front of him as though surprised to see it there. "Oh. Quite satisfactory. Thank you."

Thank God, the main course arrived and they all turned their attention to their food. The relative quiet allowed Burke a moment with her thoughts.

Captain Northrup had something weighing him down.

Something fishy was happening with the Cadwalladers.

Something was killing folks aboard the *Diversion*.

She needed to find something to bring Stanley back.

That was far too many somethings.

Don't forget, something is following Greg, her pesky inner voice reminded her.

She rubbed an achy spot on her forehead with her fingertips. A sharp burst of pain on her shin snapped her out of her musing. Her attention snapped to Richard, who was staring at her with bug eyes.

She lifted a brow in silent question.

He jerked his head to one side.

She looked in that direction. Julia sipped her drink and watched Captain Northrup with a man-eating grin.

Burke shrugged at Richard. Not every female predator was a literal monster.

Richard repeated the weird little jerk in Julia's direction.

"That handsome young boy is singing again tonight. We should go see him," Annie said. "Anyone care to join us?"

"Isaac? I adore him. He's a spicy little hor d'oeuvre," Julia said. She looked at Richard and licked her lips. "Will you join us, Richard?"

Ed chuckled.

"My grandfather and Stanley and I have plans already," Burke said.

Red-faced and sweating, Richard appeared to be on the verge of a stroke. "Maybe we should go."

"I thought we'd already agreed on something else for the evening." Burke prayed he'd get her message. She had zero intention of going to another of Isaac's shows.

"We'll pick a big table in case you change your mind," Annie promised. Then they said the polite things people say when parting ways and Julie and the Santoses trooped away in the direction of the main lobby.

Richard threw up his hands. "Can't you take a hint?"

"What's your problem?" Burke asked.

"That woman is a witch!"

Burke rolled her eyes. "Grandpa, just because she—"

"She's a witch!"

Luca drew up next to them. His razor-thin eyebrows slashed downward over his narrow eyes. "Is everyone content here?"

Burke assured him they were fine and he backed away from the table with obvious reluctance.

"What's gotten into you?" Burke asked. "You've been acting weird all night."

Richard turned his chair so he could lean in close. He dropped his voice, "Listen. That woman is a witch. I know it. I know it."

"It's not likely. Witches tend to be much more grounded. Sometimes literally. They draw power from the earth," Stanley said.

A little thrill zipped through Burke's heart. He'd offered an opinion. That had to be a good sign.

Richard shook his head. "Not all of them. I read about one in that book of yours. She lived on a riverbank and commanded water demons."

"True, not all," Stanley agreed.

"She's a witch. She's the killer. I know it," Richard insisted.

"Why do you think that?" Burke asked.

Richard drew back. His gaze darted down and to the left. "I just know it."

"Grandpa?"

"Can't you trust me?"

"You're mistaken," Stanley said.

Richard pushed his dentures around the inside of his mouth with his tongue. "Who died and made you a know-it-all?"

Stanley met his gaze with an utterly bland expression. "Everyone died, Richard. Everyone I've ever known."

Damn. So much for good signs.

Richard slumped. "Today when I was at the pool, she showed up. She got in the water and..." He took a sudden interest in the pattern on the tablecloth.

Stanley's eyes swam with tears.

Burke pinched the bridge of her nose. "What did she do, Grandpa?"

He didn't look at her. "She came onto me. Hard."

Her lips twitched.

Richard's head snapped up. "Don't you laugh at me."

There wasn't a chance in Heaven or Earth she could have buried her smile, but she did manage to stop short of actual laughter. "Just because a woman makes a pass at you doesn't mean she's The Devil."

Stanley flinched.

Crap! Could she have found a worse choice of words? She took a deep breath and tried again, "She's just forward, Grandpa."

He shook his head. "It ain't like that. It ain't natural. I'm telling you. If I hadn't run away, I'd be dead now. I know it."

The words hung there waiting for a response. Around them, the wait staff began clearing tables and moving chairs.

"Maybe I'm wrong. Maybe I'm dumber than a box of rocks." He met her eyes. "But what if I'm right? She went to the show with those two old farts. If I'm right, they're dead by morning."

Burke deflated. "What do you want to do? We can't exactly march into the lobby and stab her with an iron dagger."

"Iron doesn't hurt witches," Stanley mumbled.

Richard twisted his hands together. "We should at least follow them, make sure they're okay. That old fart'd drive a wooden Indian crazy, but he don't deserve to go out as some witch's sacrifice."

Burke knew when she'd been defeated. She was going to see the Prince impersonator again, whether she wanted to or not.

CHAPTER THIRTEEN

Gordon

GORDON HAD WRITTEN DOWN EVERY MINUTE DETAIL OF THE circumstances of each of the three deaths on index cards and lay them out on his desk. It looked like he was trying to do his own tarot reading. He sought out matching words.

Male.

First Class Passenger.

Smile.

He shuffled the cards around. Two of the men died on the ship. One was found in a secluded spot on land.

This drama was like reincarnation. He was doomed to live this mystery over and over every week until he learned something from it.

He found a roll of antacids in his desk drawer and popped one into his mouth while he studied.

The captain had a point about the new hires. Gordon felt the need to be extra cautious, all things considered, but the fact of the matter was that no one who'd been on the ship less than several months could possibly have anything to do with the deaths.

Was it sabotage? The *Diversion's* luxurious design had received a lot of press. He guessed the folks in charge at some of the other cruise lines were less than thrilled about that. Maybe the killer wasn't one person. Maybe a series of saboteurs were poisoning the *Diversion's* wealthiest guests in an attempt to drive the cruise line out of business.

He shuffled the cards again.

The deaths didn't feel like corporate espionage. It felt like a game. Someone killed people for the sheer pleasure of it.

The antacid did little to settle his churning stomach.

A pattern almost emerged. Ike's name appeared just after the first death, and right before the second. Not the third, though. He'd been with Gordon at the time the doc estimated the guy kicked the bucket. Besides, no one had ever loved their job like Ike. He'd never do anything to endanger his position aboard the *Diversion*.

Gordon's gaze drew a line between a single name that repeated three times.

Captain Northrup ate with the first guy just before he was killed.

Captain Northrup took a rare, unusual, unexplained shore leave the day the second man died.

Captain Northrup was seen outside the bar with the third vic less than thirty minutes before his wife placed the emergency call.

Captain Northrup who smiled too much, had too much money, and never seemed as interested as he should be in solving the mystery surrounding the passengers in his care.

Gordon scooped the cards into a sloppy pile and dumped

them on one side of his desk. He spread the cards from the previous week's journey across the desktop.

The captain's name was not specifically mentioned in connection with every event, but with enough of them to make Gordon's heart beat a little faster. He muttered a string of curses under his breath. Could it be him, really? Or was Gordon's judgment clouded by a general dislike of the man?

He needed a second opinion, but who could he trust? Certainly, none of the idiots who were supposed to be his assistants.

Ike.

Ike saw everything. He knew everything. He loved the *Diversion* like a father loves his child.

Gordon picked up the phone and made a call.

IKE'S OFFICE WAS A STARK CONTRAST TO GORDON'S. FOR one, he had the luxury of a window—a tiny one, and oddly placed too close to the floor, but it did offer a little natural light and a glimpse of the water. Rather than clean, bare walls, this room was covered in posters, racks of brochures, and shelves stacked high with everything from board games to cricket bats. Half a dozen signed photographs showed Ike grinning next to politicians and movie stars who'd aged out of the game. Under stacks of three-ring binders, a calendar, a dirty coffee cup, and a corporate coffee mug stuffed full of pens, it was difficult to make out the actual desktop.

The big man sat with his desk chair tipped back. His left arm lay across his stomach and he rubbed his smooth-shaven chin with the fingers of his right hand. "I wish I could help, Gordon. You have no idea how much I wish that. The situation, as far as I can ascertain, is every bit as dire as one would think. Stocks are down. The media's buzzing about. Word is out that something is wrong on this ship and people are afraid."

Gordon perched on the edge of the single guest chair. "So far, we've given no indication to anyone anywhere that these deaths are anything other than natural."

Ike leaned forward and rested his forearms on the desk. The chair creaked under his immense weight. "But you're convinced they're not."

"I am."

He nodded. For the first time ever, Gordon noticed dark circles under the man's eyes. "And you say the captain is the only person you can connect to every crime."

"It's not a connection exactly, certainly nothing that I could ever offer to a judge to get a warrant. It's a coincidence. He pops up too close, too often, and sometimes—like the other day when the vic was found on the beach—he didn't belong there."

Ike chewed on his lip. His gaze wandered toward the window. "It's not the captain."

Gordon scooted farther forward, so his butt barely touched the chair and his knees bumped the front of the desk. "Why do you say that?"

He continued to avoid Gordon's eye. "I just know. It can't be him."

"Tell me why," Gordon pushed.

"He's not powerful enough."

What the hell is that supposed to mean?

Gordon didn't ask aloud. He waited. He could be good at waiting when he needed to be.

Ike shook his head. "I can't explain it. I just know."

"The way I just know something's wrong," Gordon said.

"No. It's not instinct that I'm talking about. I'm telling you that it takes a powerful human to intentionally take a life. It's not a healthy power. It has nothing to do with physical strength. It's something else. Maybe in the heat of the moment, Roy could pull a trigger, but the way those people died—whatever this is—it's not him. Not directly, anyway."

"Not directly, but maybe he's part of something?"

The big man's chin quivered and, for one horrified second, Gordon wondered if he would burst into tears. Thank God, he pulled himself together and squared his shoulders. "I don't know. I wish I did. I wish we had someone here who..."

Gordon waited again, but it didn't work this time. "Someone who?"

Ike shrugged. "Someone who could see what we can't see."

"Yeah." He stood to leave. "Well, if you get any great flashes of insight, you let me know, hear?"

"I'll do that, Gordon. I hope with all my heart you find a way to put a stop to this."

Gordon walked out thinking about the two FBI agents. Was it time to ask for some real help or would that make matters worse? Given the chance, he'd be happy to pay good money for a working crystal ball so he could get some real answers for a change.

CHAPTER FOURTEEN

Richard

RICHARD SPOTTED THE SANTOSES AND THE WITCH RIGHT UP front. Everyone appeared to be alive and functional. He breathed a sigh of relief. Obviously, Burke and Stanley thought he was some sort of lunatic and they were patronizing him by coming to the show. So be it. At least, nobody would die that night.

Burke picked a table in the darkest shadows at the back of the room. Richard guessed her choice had more to do with hiding from the little man on stage than conducting a covert operation. Fine with him. Whatever worked.

A waitress in a black dress that hugged her like a second skin offered to fetch their drinks. Richard wondered that she had the strength to carry trays full of beverages. She was so skinny she probably had to run circles in the shower to get wet. He ordered a cup of coffee. Stanley asked for Earl Grey tea and Burke said she'd have water. The waitress sashayed away from them as if offended by their non-alcoholic preferences.

On stage, Isaac sang about raspberry berets.

Burke watched Julia.

Richard watched Burke.

Stanley stared at nothing.

The girl returned with his coffee and he sort of wished he'd ordered something stronger. "I ain't crazy," he said after the waitress left.

"I don't think you're crazy," Burke said.

"But you think I'm wrong."

When she looked at him, he noticed the slump of her shoulders. "I keep thinking about the Cadwalladers."

Whatever he'd expected her to say, that wasn't it. "What about them?"

"Why're they beat up?"

Richard considered the question. His mind offered random static. "I know what Ed Santos thinks."

"I'm pretty sure the only things Ed Santos thinks about are sex and drugs," Burke said.

Richard couldn't argue with that. "How do you think he ended up with a dame like Annie?"

"Love is mysterious," Burke said.

They sat through the rest of the show, an hour and a half of songs Richard couldn't name. Ed drank until he sat tilted sideways in his chair. Annie kept her hands folded primly on the table before her. Julia sipped her cocktail, chatted with the staff and waved at fellow passengers as they meandered in and out of the lounge. Richard found the evening equally exciting as watching paint dry.

The singer took his final bows and the house lights brightened just enough to signal the end of the show. Julia pushed her chair away from the table and stood. Richard poked Burke. "There she goes."

Ed and Annie stayed in their seats.

"I saw you from stage."

Richard and Burke jumped. They'd both been so focused on Julia, neither of them noticed Isaac's approach. Stanley showed as much emotion as a lump of wet clay.

"I'm so happy you came back. I've been thinking of you." He pulled out the chair next to Burke and perched on the edge of it.

She gave a half-hearted attempt at a smile. "It was a great show, but we were just leaving."

An idea burst like a road flare in Richard's mind. "No, we should stay."

Burke turned her hands palms-up. "I thought you had a plan in mind for the evening." Her gaze darted in the direction Julia had gone.

He gestured toward the Santoses. "Maybe I was wrong. Everything seems fine now."

She threw up her hands.

Isaac leaned toward her. "He's right. You should stay."

"We need your help," Richard said.

Everyone focused on him.

He fidgeted. "You've worked on this ship a while, right?"

"A while, yes." He looked at Burke again. "It's a fantastic life, but lonely. With the right woman at my side, I'd be Adam in paradise."

"Adam's woman led him astray," Burke said.

"I bet he never regretted it." Isaac grinned at her.

Richard jumped in before crap got so deep he'd need a shovel and hip waders. "Tell us what you know about Julia Domina."

The little man threw back his head and laughed. "That old girl? She's a regular player. I mean, at home, I knew some guys who made the rounds, but I never met anyone like Julia. She changes her men more often than she changes her jewelry."

"Have you ever noticed anything strange about her?" Richard asked.

Isaac roared with laughter. "That lady is so far from normal, I'd be suspicious if she ever did anything regular."

"Far from normal in what way?" Burke asked.

Isaac shook his head. He waved a finger at the rail-thin waitress and she nodded. "She's just crazy, you know? The best kind of crazy. I bet she was at Woodstock, butt-naked and smoking a blunt while Hendrix played. Or if not that, sleeping with some high-end diplomat in North Vietnam for intel. I guarantee, she never worked the sales counter at Macy's and worried where the rent money would come from. Ask her what she thinks of Camilla Parker Bowles and I bet she'd laugh and tell you a story that included Prince Charles and his royal scepter, if you catch my drift."

Richard's brain stumbled over the idea that a woman who'd slept with Prince Charles might want to sleep with him. The face of his high school track coach popped into mind and admonished him to keep his fly shut. *If you get in the back seat with some fast girl, you might as well be in the back seat with every guy she's ever been with.* So, if he went to bed with Julia, did that mean he could say he'd made it with the Prince of England? He blinked and ordered himself to focus. "Do you think she's a monster?"

The skinny waitress brought a bottle of beer and a glass of water and placed them on the table in front of Isaac. She blushed and hustled off without a word. Isaac drained half the beer in a single go. "Nah. She's not bad. Just wild. Maybe we should all be so free."

"Do you think she has anything to do with the weird deaths on the ship?" Burke asked.

Richard approved. The kid was on the same wavelength as him. This was a prime opportunity to pump an employee for first-hand info about the situation.

Isaac's plucked-and-drawn eyebrows shot up. "Julia? Why would you think that?"

"Those deaths are weird," Burke said.

The singer told them that he agreed completely. "Not just weird, but eerie as hell. Seems like every day another old geezer keels over, grinning ear to ear. They keep them in the ship's morgue and the doc says it's natural causes, but I hear it from reliable sources that when he says 'natural causes,' what he actually means is, 'I don't have the slightest idea what's going on here.' Healthy people don't drop dead for no reason, not even super-old healthy people, and if they do, they're surely not happy about it." He finished his beer and picked up the water glass. "Why are you asking these questions anyway?"

"We're FBI," Burke said.

Isaac choked on his water. "All of you?"

Richard glanced at his companions. Which of them seemed unbelievable as an FBI agent?

Stanley traced the little blue anchor on his paper napkin with one fingertip.

It had to be him.

"All of us," Burke said. "We're on vacation, but once a cop, always a cop, right? Something smells bad on this boat."

Isaac drank his water and thought it over. Finally, he said, "I bet you don't know the half of it." He glanced at his watch. "Come on. There's something I want to show you."

✡

THE DAY BEFORE, RICHARD HAD TOLD BURKE HE'D explored every part of the ship, but he hadn't really had any concept of how many areas were off limits to passengers. Isaac led them into a catacomb of low-ceilinged hallways where their steps echoed around them with such intensity, the sound resembled that of a marching army.

Burke and Isaac walked side-by-side. In her high-heeled sandals, she stood a full head taller than him. She glided with long graceful strides, head high, shoulders back—a woman who moved through the world as a force to be reckoned with. The rock star wannabe sashayed with little mincing steps. Despite their differences, they looked weirdly right together, a wolf and a bobcat with an alliance.

Stanley kept pace with them, leaning heavily on his cane. He hunched over as if he walked against a strong wind.

Richard remembered Stanley without his shadow. He'd been so light and free, he literally started turning into light itself. Now that he had his darkness attached again, he resembled Atlas, bowed under the immeasurable weight of the sky. Were they wrong to put him back together? Seemed like fading to stardust was a better fate than being crushed under the burden of life's sorrows. If they failed, would Stanley simply—

"Here." Isaac stopped in front of a white door with a little gray sign that read, *Storage-1015*. He glanced in both directions and swiped a little plastic card over a black rectangle above the doorknob. Something beeped and they piled into a closet the size of an average bathroom. Overhead fluorescents lent a sickly yellow ambiance.

Isaac pointed at a shelf bearing three white cardboard

boxes, each with a name scrawled across the front in black permanent marker. "Those are the items that were on the bodies at the time of death."

"How do you even know about this?" Burke asked.

"There are no secrets when you're trapped on a boat with your co-workers."

Stanly reached up and ran a hand across one of the names. "There are always secrets, my friend. Always."

Burke pulled down a box, set it on the floor, and squatted to lift the lid. The overhead light revealed a set of clothing, a little baggie with some jewelry, a wallet, and a belt. "It was a long walk to look at a dead man's Chinos."

Isaac raised an eyebrow and leaned in close to her. "I'm not showing you what's there. I'm showing you what isn't."

They peered into the cardboard rectangle and puzzled over that.

Isaac put his hands on his hips and shook his head. "Great detectives from the FBI, eh? Shoes, people. There are no shoes."

Richard scratched his head. "He died in bed, right? So, no shoes. Makes sense to me."

"But who lays down in bed with their wallet and belt?" Burke asked.

Isaac made a finger gun and shot it in her direction. "Exactamundo."

The door swung open and everyone pivoted in that direction.

Ike, the activities director, filled the space, blocking most of the light from the hallway. Judging by the little yelp he let out, he was as surprised to see them as they were to see him. "What are you doing?"

Richard reached into his pocket and produced his FBI badge.

Ike shook his head. "You're investigating? What's to investigate?"

"A lot of people die on this ship," Burke said.

"People die on cruise ships. Our guests tend to be—"

"We're hunters," Stanley said.

Richard and Burke gaped at him. The old peacock had to be locked up. He was a danger to himself and others.

"Hunters." Ike's Adam's apple bobbed. He took a step back.

"We're not here for you," Stanley said.

Ike's gaze locked on Stanley's. "You know who I am?"

"Not really, but I'm guessing you're not human."

"What gave me away?"

"Nothing anyone else would notice. You move too fast. You remember too well."

Richard closed his mouth and tried to process.

A smile spread across Ike's face. "I knew there was something about you."

Stanley gave a little bow as if responding to a compliment from the Queen of England.

Isaac's head spun from one side to the other. "What are you talking about? Who's not human? What do you mean, you're hunters?"

"He's an innocent," Stanley told Ike.

Ike nodded.

Isaac looked at Burke. "I'm not that innocent."

She ignored him and stood up from her squat beside the box. "What are you?"

Ike studied the group, peeked out into the hallway, and

apparently came to some kind of conclusion. "Not here. Let's go to my room. It's safer there."

Richard huffed. "People are dying on this ship and you want us to go to your room with you? I don't think so, Monster."

Ike gazed at him with big, sad, puppy-dog eyes. "I'm not a monster. I haven't hurt anyone. Please come with me. I'll tell you everything I know." His gargantuan shoulders slumped. "If only I had more to tell. If you're hunters, maybe you can figure out what I'm missing."

Burke agreed for the group.

Richard seriously doubted the kid's judgment, but he kept that opinion to himself. If they were going into a monster's lair, they were going in together.

DEEP IN THE BOWELS OF THE SHIP, THE ROAR OF THE engines thrummed inside Richard's bones, and he sensed the ocean pressing in from every side, seeking entrance to the belly of this beast cleaving the water. Ike held open the door to a tiny room that resembled the inside of an aluminum lunchbox. Burke stood with her back against the wall. Stanley drooped, a soggy noodle, against the wall next to her. Isaac flounced into one of four cheap plastic chairs the color of moldy green olives. He folded his hands on the table. "All this talk of monsters and hunters. Color me intrigued."

Ike pulled the door shut. "I'm not a monster," he said again.

"You keep saying that," Burke said.

Ike pulled out one of the remaining chairs and lowered himself into it. His long legs sprawled across the space between the chair and the table. He propped his elbows on his knees and pressed his palms together. "My name is Ikatere." He looked around at them as though waiting for some kind of acknowledgment, but the others must have been as clueless as Richard because they didn't respond, either. Ikatere leaned back and rubbed a hand across his smooth scalp. "I am the god of the sea."

Burke crossed her arms. "You're God."

"Little g," Ike said.

"And you took a job on a cruise ship?" Richard asked.

The supposed god suddenly became fascinated by the patterns in the concrete on the floor. "Times aren't what they once were."

Isaac raised a hand as if swearing to his testimony in court. "You don't need to tell a brother that, my friend. I am a believer. The gods are not dead. I hope, myself, to walk among you one of these days."

"There are no more sacrifices," Stanley said. "No blood to fuel you." He said it with as much passion as if remarking that the lawnmower had run out of gas.

Ike's head snapped up. "It wasn't bad. It was beautiful. The sacrifices brought no pain. They sent up dances and songs. They ate the fruit of the land and fed us on their gratitude."

"Must have been the sixties," Isaac mused.

"Us?" Burke asked.

The little-g god nodded. "My brothers and I knew the warm waters of Earth before man climbed down from the treetops. But I...we...it's just that... Well, you people seem so reasonable. I'm sure you never had some kind of misunderstanding that led to Thanksgiving Dinner cage-matches, but my family seems prone to drama."

"I wouldn't'a guessed," Richard said.

"Fury like my brother's has never been seen on this planet. When he raised his wrath, I took my children and fled to the sea. I haven't been on land since, but the ocean is a lonely place. I mean, dolphins are hospitable, but they're insufferable pranksters. The merpeople are cliquey. You wouldn't believe how bad it is, and sharks—well, sharks are just assholes."

Richard scowled. What kind of freaky hippy dippy god did they stumble into anyway? Hey! He stood straighter. "I was right."

All eyes turned on him. He grinned. "I was right. We were led here because there's a case."

Burke's lips twitched. "Yes, Grandpa. You were right."

Richard slipped his hands into his pockets and rocked on his toes. He didn't say *I told you so,* even though he very well could have. He'd grown as a person in the past year.

Ike cleared his throat and went on, "I got lonely, so I took this job. It's fantastic." He looked up at Stanley and his brown cheeks deepened to bronze. "I meet the most interesting people." He leaned forward as if he could barely resist the urge to fall at Stanley's feet. "I find you fascinating, Stanley. The first moment I saw you, I sensed a power so old it reminded me of our days in the gardens of Paradise. You are wounded, but..." His gaze traveled down Stanley's body and up again. He shivered. "You are so very, very powerful."

Burke cleared her throat. "You were telling us how you're not a monster."

"I'm not." He raised a hand. "I swear it. I'm a vegetarian. I don't even make waves. That's my brother."

Isaac laughed. "Brother, this is some kind of wild story."

"It's not a story. I am Ikatere, god of the sea."

"And I'm prince of the purple stripe in the rainbow."

Ike raised his right hand and snapped his fingers. His body

transformed into water, a humanoid droplet from Heaven's biggest faucet. A low gurgle issued from the top of the humanoid H_2O. "I am Ikatere, god of the sea."

There came the sound of a bubble popping, and Ike stood before his chair, solid and dry.

Isaac's mouth dropped open, shut, opened again.

"Hush now, if you will. I need to speak with these hunters."

Ike sat down again. "If I go to land, my brother will kill me. If I return to the sea, I'll die of boredom. I've found joy on this ship. I have found safety. I'm not about to jeopardize everything I've gained by offing humans. What purpose would that serve me?"

"If you're not killing these people, then who is?" Burke asked.

Isaac made a noise like a frightened puppy.

"I can't figure it out." He stood and walked around the back of his chair. "My first thought was a witch."

"Can you be sure it isn't?" Richard asked.

"Witches kill for revenge, for power, for wealth. I've looked at every angle and these victims only have two things in common. They're all men, and they were all passengers on this ship. They had no business or personal connections, not within two generations."

"Couldn't a witch live longer than two generations?" Burke asked.

Ike shrugged. "Sure, but that's a special kind of angry. If a witch was that mad at you, you'd be dead before you had time to make babies who lived long enough to make babies old enough to make babies. You know what I'm saying?"

Richard puzzled over that statement long enough that, when he tuned into the conversation again, Ike had moved on.

"... shifter of any kind because the killings don't seem to be related in any way to the moon cycle, and not a vampire because they still have their blood. I thought maybe some sort of vengeful spirit—"

"That can't be it," Richard said. "There ain't so much as a warble of EMF on this raft."

Ike nodded.

"Another god?" Burke asked.

"I'd know that kind of power," Ike said.

Stanley staggered toward a chair and dropped into it. "Shadow demons."

Burke knelt next to him. "This isn't the same, Stanley. It's okay. This is different."

Ike chewed his nail. "I don't know what to do."

Richard had heard enough. "It's a witch, I tell you. Can't be nothing else and I know who it is, too."

"What? Who?" Ike surged to his feet.

"That dame Julia. She's a witch."

"How do you know?" Ike asked.

Burke rolled her eyes. "She hit on him and now he thinks she's evil incarnate."

"Don't nobody like a smart a—"

"She's not a witch," Ike said. "She's been on this ship for months. No spells, no incense, no special interest in herbs or crystals. She's less witchy than Stanley with his aura that's all shiny and extra."

Richard crossed his arms and pressed his lips together. If they thought he was a fool, so be it, but he would not be holding in his I-told-you-so's anymore when they learned the truth.

Burke rose, but kept one hand on Stanley's shoulder. "Maybe she's not a witch, but I bet a witch would know what this is. This is the kind of death and destruction they traffic in."

"There are no witches on this boat. I guarantee it," Ike said.

Burke tapped one long nail against the tabletop. "Maybe not, but we'll have a chance to get off this boat in eight hours or so, and I'd bet dollars to donuts, there's a witch somewhere in the Dominican Republic."

Stanley clutched his cane close to his chest like a teddy bear. "Swing a dead cat in the Dominican Republic and you're likely to hit a witch."

Isaac twisted the hem of his purple velvet jacket between his bejeweled fingers. "That's disgusting. What is wrong with you people? You're all sick and weird."

Burke winked at him. "You seriously have no idea."

CHAPTER FIFTEEN

Burke

BURKE STRUGGLED TO SQUELCH THE HINT OF embarrassment festering in her belly, no matter that cruise ship concierges answered requests ranging from the mundane to the truly bizarre on a daily basis. Her inquiry unquestionably ranked on the circus-freak end of the scale, and hours of tossing and turning, trying to come up with a different idea had yielded as much fruit as a citrus orchard in Antarctica. She strove to look as normal and unthreatening as possible to make up for the absurdity of her words. "I need to find a witch."

Nikki's wide, lovely smile never faltered, but her long, dark, most-likely-fake lashes fluttered as if by doing so they might filter out the nonsense of the request. "I'm not sure if I have any witches listed in my visitor information binders."

Burke forced a laugh. "I know. It's an unusual request. And I'm sure there's no officially correct response, but I could really use your help. Ike told me you're from the Dominican Republic."

"That's right."

"He said you lived in Puerto Plata for most of your life."

Her smile started to take on a strained look. "I did, but I'm not sure Ike has the right to share personal information about me."

Burke glanced around to make sure no one lingered close enough to overhear. "Please don't be angry with him. Look, I can't tell you all the details. You wouldn't believe me if I did, but this is important. Surely, you've met someone who dabbles."

"There are a great many unfortunate stereotypes about the Dominican people."

"I'm not trying to stereotype. I need to find someone who can help me figure out a solution to a very serious, very dangerous problem."

The woman shifted from one foot to the other. "I can't tell you where to find a witch."

Reverse psychology had to be worth a shot. After all, she had nothing so there was nothing to be lost. "I understand. Thank you for your time." Burke turned to leave.

"I can't tell you where to find a witch," Nikki said again, "but I know a shop you might be interested in."

Burke looked back at the other woman.

"They sell occult items. Crystals, charms, stuff like that."

Hope bloomed at the unhalting pace of a dandelion in spring. "I'm listening."

"It's tourist stuff. Like I said, there are stereotypes. Some of the locals use them to their advantage."

"Clever locals."

Nikki shrugged. "Clever. Greedy. Desperate. Depends on how you look at it."

"But you think I can find answers there?"

The woman held Burke's gaze for a long time. She seemed to be trying to work out whether or not Burke was playing her for a fool. "The shop is for tourists, but one of the guys that supplies them..." She turned her attention to straightening a row of tidy brochures. "Ask for Bob. If they know where he is, and mind you, they might not, be sure to tell him Nikki gave you his name. He can be a little cagey."

"Got it. Bob. Thank you. This means a lot to me."

The woman looked at her again. "You might not be thanking me after you meet Bob."

TAKING A BREATH IN THE DOMINICAN REPUBLIC WAS LIKE trying to suck air through a wool blanket soaked in hot water. Burke gave thanks to the gods of fashion that she'd shaved off her hair. Her thick, curly mane would have looked like so much tangled shrubbery in such intense humidity.

A man called out from the curb, "Tour of the city? My taxi has air conditioning. Free bottled water." The driver was built of spheres. He had a perfectly round head with close-cropped hair that curled into miniscule circles. A shirt with wide pink and white horizontal stripes stretched across shoulders the size and shape of grapefruits and a little round belly. A wide smile revealed rounded white teeth. He gestured toward a box-shaped gray minivan and Burke couldn't help thinking of the old adage about round pegs and square holes.

She handed him the slip of paper Nikki had given her. "Can you take us here?"

"Of course, of course." He winked. "I warn you, though, the Christians in America be mad at you if they know you visit this place."

"I'll risk it," she told him.

He shrugged his citrine shoulders. "You are brave, lady. Are the old men coming, too?"

She looked back at her grandfather and Stanley and was reminded of two little boys waiting on the sidewalk for their mother. "Yes. We're all together."

She tucked Stanley into the front seat, then she and Richard piled into the back and the driver headed southeast into the heart of the city.

THE SHOP WAS HOUSED INSIDE A LITTLE LAVENDER SHACK with a rusted tin roof. Crystals of varying shades dangled between the iron bars that covered the windows in lieu of glass. A large painted rock propped open the door. A spider the approximate size of Burke's hand perched atop the rock, watching the world go by. The thing had as much thick black hair as young Elvis Presley. It waved its hideous front legs at them as if welcoming them. The three hunters stepped wide of the rock and scooted through the doorway.

If Willy Wonka had gone into the black arts rather than candy making, he might have had a shop like "The Five Pointed Star." Various tiny skulls and mummified paws filled an entire wall of shelves. Shrunken heads—presumably replicas, but Burke had learned never to put too much weight in an assumption—dangled from the ends of long black lengths of yarn. In front of the windows, a thousand more crystals, some polished and cut, others cloudy and rough, cast rainbow light over the room that had been painted in shades of pink and purple. A young woman sat on a turquoise stool behind a scarred wooden table. She'd tied a yellow scarf over her long, straight, cocoa-powder hair and hung orange hoops as large as bracelets from her earlobes. Her yellow cotton dress draped full breasts that defied gravity despite an obvious lack of undergarments. She shuffled a deck of tarot cards through fingers covered in sparkling silver rings.

Both men grinned at her.

She met their stares with enormous green eyes that twinkled in the prismatic light. Her full pink lips curled into a smile. "How may I help you?"

Burke stepped in front of the men before they said something stupid. "We're looking for Bob."

The woman took Burke's measure. She brushed a strand of hair from her face. "As you can see, Bob is not here." Her tractor-beam eyes focused on the men again.

The two of them inched closer to her.

Burke rolled her eyes. "Do you know where we can find him?"

"You are absolutely fascinating," she said to Stanley.

Stanley tipped his hat. "As are you, my dear."

"What have you seen?" she asked.

Stanley turned to look at a display of tiny glass vials. "Everything," he answered.

The girl chewed her bottom lip.

Richard stepped up next to Burke. "So, what about Bob?"

"Bob keeps his own schedule."

"Are you saying you don't know where to find him?" Burke asked.

She placed the stack of cards on the table and cut the deck. "Perhaps the cards will tell you."

"The cards," Burke repeated.

"The cards reveal all kinds of information."

Burke crossed her arms. "And how much does it cost to have you read the cards?"

"Thirty dollars."

Stanley wandered toward the door. Burke gestured for her grandfather to keep an eye on him. It didn't take any great stretch of imagination to picture him drifting into the heart of the city one slow, shuffling step after another. She tossed thirty dollars on the table.

The woman flipped a card over without looking at it. "Bob's next door. He lives there."

Burke managed to bite down on the retort that tried to escape her lips. She forced a smile. "Got that from the cards, did you?"

The woman winked at her. "Girl's gotta make a living. We don't grow the American money trees in these parts."

Burke and her entourage paraded out the door and across the scrappy mess of a yard to the little yellow house next door. Two men sat on the steps eating pineapple from a wooden bowl big enough to bath a child in.

The guy on the left brushed a drop of pineapple juice from his black tank top. Thin braids hung like dead snakes from his scalp. "What you need, pretty lady?"

"Are you Bob?" she asked.

"No." He popped a chunk of pineapple into his mouth. "You want some pineapple?"

Burke closed her eyes and counted to three. She looked to the guy on the right, an adult in a twelve-year-old's body. A soccer jersey hung from his slight frame. He held the bowl on his skinny legs. "Bob?"

"Who are you, pretty lady?"

"My name is Burke." She introduced her grandfather and Stanley, who stood half a step behind her on her right-hand side. "We're passengers on the *Diversion*. Nikki told me Bob might be able to help me."

The guy in black burst into great guffaws, slapping his thighs and pointing at the little guy. "Nikki sent them!"

The smaller man ignored his companion. "What that she-devil think I can help you with?"

"So, you are Bob?" she asked.

"I am."

Burke wiped away the sweat beading her brow before it could drip into her eyes and blind her. "I was under the impression you and Nikki are friends."

"I enjoy her very much," he said.

"You just called her a she-devil."

The left end of his mouth curled up. "That's why I enjoy her."

Richard made a noise that might have been a laugh or a sign of intestinal distress. It wasn't always easy to tell with him. Stanley stared into space as if enthralled in a movie no one else could see.

"I need the help of a witch," Burke said.

The guy in black started laughing again. He stood up and staggered away in a fit of great, gasping hilarity.

"Have some pineapple," Bob suggested.

"No, thank you. Can you help me?"

"I'm not sure yet. Sit. Have some pineapple."

"Really, I'm fine. We're a little short on time," Burke said.

Bob enjoyed another chunk of fruit. "This is the island, pretty lady. Time has no meaning here."

"We're Americans. We schedule our toilet breaks," Richard said.

Bob shook his head and tsked. "Poor Americans. You are

slaves, every last one. Land of the free. Bah! Sit. Eat the fruit. Enjoy the sun."

"I ain't a slave because I choose to be punctual," Richard said. "It's my choice. If I wanted to sit in the sun all day eating pineapple and doing nothin', I could. I'd rather be doing something."

"So, you are a human doing and not a human being?"

"Boy, you're as crazy as a Baptist in a brothel."

Bob grinned. "At least that crazy, old man. Sit. Eat the pineapple."

Richard plopped down on the step with a great deal of groaning and cracking joints. He chose a piece of fruit from the bowl and mashed it up between his ill-fitting dentures. "That ain't half bad."

"Not even half," Bob agreed. "Now we've eaten together. I can call you friend, and I will help you, but don't you tell Nikki I helped you because of her. She don't need her head to get no bigger. What do you want?"

Burke wiped away more sweat. No wonder people on this island didn't fuss over time. The heat was enough to strip away a person's will to do anything except...well...except sit around eating fruit. "We're hunters," Burke said.

Bob's eyes narrowed. He tensed to run.

"Wait. We've got nothing against you."

He kept his gaze steady on Burke. "Maybe I've got something against you. You just walk into my yard and tell me you're a bunch of killers?"

"We only kill monsters," Richard told him.

"In a hunter's mind, there's a fine line between a monster and a witch."

"We just told you, we need you. Why would we kill you?" Burke asked.

He hesitated. "What do you want?"

"People are dying on the ship," Burke said.

"Death is everywhere. Every living thing is dying," Stanley muttered.

They all stared at him. He watched a butterfly fluttering from flower to flower.

Burke took a deep breath of soggy air to try to focus her thoughts. "People are dying on the ship," she said again. "They're declared natural deaths, heart attacks mostly, but they seem fishy."

"They seem witchy," Richard said.

If they'd been sitting at a table, Burke would have kicked him in the shin. "We have no evidence of witchcraft. It could be anything. That's the problem. We don't know what it is, and we don't know how to stop it."

"You mean you don't know how to kill the thing that's causing the deaths."

"You got a problem with us killing a killer?" Richard asked.

"If a cow busted in your door and shot you dead, would it be justified?" Bob asked.

Richard opened his mouth to say something and then shut it again.

Burke was thinking of the girl next door and her helpful reading of the tarot cards. "I will pay you a hundred dollars to help us."

Bob's scrutiny left her feeling as if her soul had just been aired on a clothesline for all the neighbors to see. Finally, he said, "If you offer a hundred so casually, you can afford two hundred."

"Two hundred dollars to answer some questions?"

"Pay him," Stanley said. "It's not as if you can take it with you."

"He's wise," Bob said.

Burke cursed at all of them inside her mind, but she agreed, mostly on the grounds that it was the first time in weeks she'd heard Stanley actually make any kind of definitive statement.

"Tell me what you know for sure," Bob said.

Burke explained what the doctor had told them but left out the parts about Ike.

Bob narrowed his gaze. "That's not everything."

"It's enough for you to tell us if it's a witch that's murdering these people."

He tipped the bowl for Richard to take a piece of pineapple. "It's not a witch."

"How can you be so sure?" Richard asked.

Stanley limped over to a nearby palm tree and lowered himself to sit on the ground in the slim shade offered by the narrow leaves.

"That man's soul is sick," Bob said, watching him go.

"Let's focus on the task at hand," Burke said. The festering cancer in Stanley's soul was a subject she lacked the will to dive into, at the moment. She repeated her grandfather's question.

"No witch would kill like that. It's too random. Strangers? No connection except that they all wandered onto the cruise ship? There's no reason. No benefit."

"So, what, then?" Burke asked.

Bob tapped his broken nails against the side of the bowl. "They died smiling?"

"That's what the doctor told us."

He shook his head. "I've never seen it myself. I might be wrong. Probably am, but I read it once in the lore. A thing from the Old World. A leszy."

"A leszy can't survive out of the forest," Stanley said.

Burke looked over her shoulder at him. He seemed to have spoken to a lizard he held clasped between his hands.

"You could put that creature in your pocket and keep it alive for a long time. That don't mean your pocket is the best place for it to live. Life adapts," Bob said. He held up his hands in front of his chest. "Then again, like I said. Probably, I'm wrong."

"What does a leszy do?"

He chuckled. "It's a tickle monster."

"You yanking our chain?" Richard asked.

"I wouldn't dare," Bob assured him. "A leszy can take on the shape of any man. It lures its victims to a private location and tickles them to death, feeding its immortality on the laughter."

"Any man? Not a woman?" Richard asked.

"Only men. Leszy are male, always."

Burke rubbed her forehead with her fingertips. Maybe she'd drowned in the humidity and now she was hallucinating this new bit of ridiculousness. Why not play along? "Okay, then. How do you kill it?"

Bob rocked back and forth as if hearing a song audible to only him. "You have to turn your shoes inside out and put them back on while it's tickling you."

Richard huffed.

"You don't believe me?" Bob asked.

"I think you're two pickles short of a barrel," Richard said.

Bob chuckled. "I'm not the one picking fights with monsters."

Burke wished she could argue, but there wasn't much to say.

"A man?" Richard said.

"Ya, man. A man." Bob tipped the pineapple bowl in Richard's direction and he took another piece.

"Is there any way to make it reveal itself?" Burke asked.

Bob shrugged. "There is always a way, yes? But I am a witch and not a hunter and I'm probably wrong." He popped the final piece of fruit into his mouth and slurped the extra juice from his fingers. "Me? I'd walk away. A leszy is an old thing. It has stayed alive a long time through strength and cunning." He shrugged. "But you won't follow that advice anyway. It's not the hunter way of life."

Burke narrowed her eyes at him. "You're right. It's not. We will find a way."

The witch made a gesture in the air. "Go then and blessed be." His gaze moved to Stanley. "Hey, old man."

Stanley met his eyes.

"You have a choice to make. Not making it is a choice in itself."

"I can't," Stanley said.

Bob shook his head sadly. "Donkey got a long ear, but he don't like to hear his own story."

Stanley placed the lizard in a clump of flowers and pushed himself to his feet. "I'm tired."

"Every day's not Sunday," Bob said.

"You got a saying for everything?" Richard asked.

"Are you the pot calling the kettle black?" Bob shot back.

Burke rolled her eyes. "Thank you, Bob. Guys, we should go back. We got what we came for. We have a monster to find."

CHAPTER SIXTEEN

Richard

RICHARD STARED AT JULIA ACROSS THE ENORMOUS TRAY OF fresh fruit recently deposited on the table by Luca. The man seemed pleased as a pig in mud to present them with slices of fresh melon and pomegranate seeds. Julia had gushed over how pretty the arrangement was and selected several pieces using the silver tongs.

Richard would have sworn she was a witch. Could Bob be wrong? Could they trust a witch to out a witch? Why hadn't Stanley guessed the monster was a leszy?

He jabbed a melon square with his fork. The sweet, juicy fruit tasted like sunshine and sugar, but it had nothing on the pineapple he'd eaten earlier in the day.

Terry and Val had been prattling on since they arrived about the adventure they'd had, swimming with the dolphins.

"They're so intelligent," Val said.

"And gentle," Terry added. "They brush up against you, but never hard enough to push you around."

"You know, scientists say that dolphins are actually smarter than humans in a lot of ways," Val said.

Terry tugged on a lock of her hair. "Not smarter than you, Babe. You're the most clever girl in the world."

Julia pressed a hand to her heart. "Oh, young love. How delicious."

Val giggled and blushed.

Luca set a bowl of cucumber soup in front of Julia. "I have to agree with Ms. Domina. Listen to the laughter of the girl. It feeds the soul, no? Nothing better in the world than the sound of joy."

Richard's gaze locked on the waiter.

The sound of joy? Laughter? Feeding the soul? According to Bob, the leszy tickled people and fed on their laughter.

Richard's fork clattered against his plate.

Luca served his soup. "Is everything to your satisfaction?"

Richard tried to speak. He croaked like a frog, cleared his throat, tried again. "Fine. Fine. Hey, I was wondering. Do they ever let you go ashore?"

"Of course. I adore the islands. The food, the sheer joy of the Caribbean people, they are delights to me."

Annie piped up from the other side of the table, "The people really are lovely. One little child gave me a seashell necklace."

"You were supposed to pay for that," Ed said.

"He said it was a gift." She scooped up a spoonful of soup. "He called me 'pretty American lady.' Charming!"

Luca spread his thin arms wide and gave a little bow. "Enjoy your soup." He wove through the other diners and disappeared into the kitchen.

"Excuse me." Burke tossed her napkin on the table and practically ran out of the room toward the lobby.

"Where's she running off to like her tail's on fire?" Richard asked.

"Perhaps she needs to use the ladies' room," Stanley suggested. He sipped some soup from his spoon and gazed out the window.

Ed pushed his bowl away. "Who ever heard of cold soup?"

"I've heard of a cold fish," Annie replied, pointedly turning her back on him.

"I think it's delicious," Val gushed. "I just love flavorful vegetarian food."

"I just love you," Terry told her.

She batted her eyelashes at him and traced a long scratch on his cheek with the pad of her pointer finger. "I love you more, my squishy honeybun."

Ed waved his empty glass in the air. "Gonna need some more booze over here."

Luca rushed up from out of nowhere. "Right away, Mr. Santos. Can I get anything for anyone else?"

The tablemates agreed that everything was fantastic and they wanted for nothing.

"Then I shall return in the briefest of moments," the waiter declared.

Richard poked Stanley with his elbow. "What do you think about that guy?"

Stanley's gaze drifted around the room as if trying to figure out who Richard was talking about.

"The waiter. He seem...you know...copacetic?"

"He's very good at his job," Stanley said.

"Isn't he, though?" Julia gushed. "Luca is the finest waiter on the high seas."

"How long has he worked on this ship?" Richard asked.

Julia shrugged. "Longer than I've been aboard."

The subject of their discussion returned with Ed's fresh drink and plates of stuffed manicotti. Richard watched him serve the pasta. Why hadn't he seen it earlier? Nothing was in the correct proportions. His arms were too long for his body. His hands were too big for his arms. He had fingers slim and knobby as carrots. His nose was too straight. His smile too broad. Richard could have kicked himself for being so stupid. All this time he was so busy convincing himself that the lecherous old lady was a witch, he never even thought to pay attention to the waiter.

Luca gave his customary little bow and stepped away, but he didn't return to the kitchen as he normally did. Rather, halfway through the dining room, he abruptly changed course and departed into the lobby.

Richard considered saying something to Stanley, but the old peacock was so far gone into his own world he'd be more of a hindrance than a help. "I'm gonna check on Burke." He threw his napkin down and raced out of the room, hoping against hope he'd be able to stop the monster before anyone else died.

CHAPTER SEVENTEEN

Gordon

THE SEED IKE HAD PLANTED HAD SPROUTED FAST-GROWING roots in Gordon's mind. What if the captain was working with someone? But who? He'd stared at the cards until the words were no more than curling black splotches of ink. He asked questions of staff and guests alike. Nothing added up. Ike's job, his reputation, and the lives of the passengers entrusted into his care were hanging by a thread and he was trying to hammer square pegs into round holes.

The time had come.

Before he had a chance to overthink his plan and change his mind, he hurried to the dining room to speak with the captain.

Dinner was in full swing and the room was noisy with clanking silverware and drunken voices raised louder than necessary. He cut a straight path to the captain's table and came up behind him.

Captain Northrup made no move to acknowledge him, so

he bent down and spoke just loud enough to be heard, "I've waited as long as I can. I don't have the resources to stop these"— he glanced at the woman seated in the next chair. She made too great a show of not overhearing—"these incidents. When we reach port, I'm calling the authorities and giving them everything I have."

The captain gave a little shake of his head.

"It's the right thing to do. It's what we should have done in the first place."

Roy Northrup turned to glare at him. His mouth was fixed in a thin, straight line. He excused himself from the table and pulled Gordon to a corner away from the diners. "It'll be the ruination of every man and woman on this ship. Is that what you want? Some of these kids come here from places where only one adult out of fifty has a job. You want to be the one to send them home again?"

"I'd rather send them home broke than dead."

"No one on staff has died," he whispered through gritted teeth. "Passengers have died through no fault of ours. Do not call the authorities."

Who but a man with desperate secrets would be so adamant? Gordon felt like a fool. He should have acted faster, listened to his gut sooner. He rose to his full height. "Fine. It's on you." He turned and stalked away, fully intending to make the call regardless of the captain's wishes. He'd find another job. Or maybe he wouldn't. Maybe he'd retire and go somewhere cold and cloudy just because he could.

Sitting at the table lording over the dining room like some sort of benevolent king. Who did he think...

Wait.

The captain made it a rule to never leave the table before

every one of his VIP guests had finished and excused themselves. He'd be in the dining room for at least another hour.

Gordon had a key to every lock on the ship, including the lock on the door to the captain's cabin. An hour would be plenty of time to confirm his suspicions or calm them.

He fought the urge to jog. Whatever happened later, he didn't want anyone saying he was acting suspiciously. He had to find evidence and it had to be the kind of evidence that would stick and make a judge listen. A bunch of grinning dead men with bad hearts and a gut instinct would get him nowhere. He looked at his watch and nodded. Damn, but it felt good to finally be doing something.

CHAPTER EIGHTEEN

Burke

BURKE SAT AT THE DINNER TABLE NEXT TO HER grandfather and watched Gordon Westchester. He moved with a lion's grace, quick and powerful, aware of every inch of his surroundings, unafraid of any of it, and bent down to speak in the captain's ear.

Captain Northrup stared straight ahead. A muscle in his jaw jumped. He shook his head.

Gordon said something else.

The captain all but dragged him to a corner and she had to strain to see them.

Burke was no lip reader, but even at this distance, she saw the words form on Gordon's mouth, "Fine. It's on you." He turned with the precision of a soldier and stalked away from the captain.

That man knew more than he was telling anyone about the things happening on board the *Diversion*, and she was going to get him to talk, whether he liked it or not. Burke tossed her napkin on the table and excused herself. She walked as fast as she could without arousing suspicion. She reached the lobby just as he swiped a key card to enter the same spartan passageway Isaac had led them into the day before.

"Mr. Westchester!"

He turned and his gaze washed over her in a tsunami of heat and desire.

Her heart fluttered in her breast. *Geez. Calm down, for Pete's sake. You're not sixteen and he's not the captain of the football team.* She swallowed hard and forced her breathing into a slower pattern, determined to give the appearance of calm.

"Can I help you?" he asked once she was close enough that he had no need to raise his voice.

"Oh, I hope so." Hot blood rushed to her cheeks. She had not meant for that to sound like a come-on line from a 1950's "B" movie.

He tilted his head as if puzzling over whether that was an honest answer, a come-on, or some kind of prank.

Burke tried again. "I'm not sure if you remember me, but I—"

"Agent Burke Martin, bored FBI agent."

"I prefer helpful."

"Yes, well, I prefer that jurisdictional boundaries and order-of-command be honored."

"I couldn't agree more," Burke said.

He raised a brow. "Really?"

"That's why I followed you when I saw you leave the dining room. I wanted to apologize."

"Apology accepted." He turned toward the door.

"Also," Burke said, a little louder than she intended.

He paused and looked back over his shoulder.

"I really am hoping you can help me."

He came back to her. "I'm listening."

"I'm not on vacation. There have been a series of interstate killings. We followed the trail and it led us here."

He narrowed his eyes on her. "You're lying."

"Am I?"

He moved closer and the scent of his cologne slipped across the space between them and booped Burke on the tip of the nose. "Whatever is happening on this ship has nothing to do with any investigation you have on the mainland."

She raised her chin. "And how, exactly, can you be so sure of that?"

"Because whatever is killing people on this ship, assuming it's not bacteria or the overly-exciting lounge shows, never stops long enough to get across state lines on the mainland."

"Where are you going right now?" she asked.

"Why would I tell you that?"

Burke matched him glare for glare. "Because you're stumped, and you're worried, and you know that every person who dies makes your hands a little bloodier. Now there is a person here who might be able to help you and you might have as much pride as a prince on parade, but you're not stupid. You know you need me."

"What about your partner?"

"We'll fill him in later," she said.

He stared into her eyes so long she began to wonder if he could see her naked soul. She fought to stand still, neither blinking nor fidgeting. Without another word, he returned to the door and swiped his card again.

Burke followed, and he made no objection.

For the second time in two days, she found herself traveling the hidden corridors of the ship. Up some stairs, up again, they climbed until they were directly below the bridge.

Gordon stopped in front of one of the doors. "This is Captain Northrup's suite."

"We're just going to march in there?" A hot lead ball dropped into Burke's stomach.

"Haven't you ever let yourself into someone's apartment before, Agent?"

Burke fumbled for words. "I...we...not without a warrant."

"I have probable cause," he said.

"Like what?"

"Like my gut. People are dying on this ship and Captain Northrup is insisting it be covered up."

"So, you think he knows what's killing them?"

The muscle in his jaw jumped. "I think he *is* what's killing them." He used a key, not a plastic card, to unlock the door and she followed him into the apartment, too stunned to speak. She'd have put Gordon himself higher up the list of suspects than Captain Northrup.

The designer of the suite had obviously intended a theme of understated luxury. Soft lighting cast a warm glow over furniture upholstered in rich faux leather. Modern, asymmetrical bookshelves hung on every wall. She'd never seen so many cabinets.

"Space is at a premium at sea," Gordon said when she mentioned it. "You store everything you can, anywhere you can, or you leave in on shore."

Burke scanned the books on the shelves—mostly modern murder-mysteries. The kitchen cabinets showed nothing out of the ordinary, unless you believe a man past middle age eating a steady diet of sugary cereal is unusual. "He's not our guy," she said.

Gordon sat in the desk chair, leafing through a stack of

paper. He continued to read as he spoke, "What makes you say that?"

Because a monster who feeds on the laughter of the doomed wouldn't worry about stocking his cabinets with Captain Crunch and Sugar Pops. "What I see in this room doesn't fit the MO of the guy we're looking for."

"What I see in this room tells a story I've been too distracted to see playing out in front of my eyes. Look at this."

She came to stand behind him and read over his shoulder. She worked hard to focus on the papers and not the flexing of the muscles in his forearms.

Rows of numbers—dollar amounts—covered the pages, each with a hand-written notation beside it.

$1468, billed $1492, + $24 – food service

$9,763, billed $10, 223, + $460 – medical supplies

$714, billed $746, +32 – laundry supplies

It went on in that way for page after page.

Burke shook her head. "I don't understand."

"He's running a nickel and dime operation."

She read the numbers again. "Billing a little more than necessary for everything and keeping the difference."

He nodded. "I'm no math whiz, but a quick glance tells me he's racked up more than thirty-five-thousand dollars this year alone."

"He's a thief, not a murderer," Burke said.

"Let's get out of here," Gordon said. "Now that I know what I'm looking for, I can find a better way to nail his ass to the wall."

"You mean a way that will actually hold up in court."

He agreed. They returned everything to the right places, slipped back into the hall, and distanced themselves from the Captain's quarters.

"There's still the little issue of a murderer on your ship," Burke pointed out once they were alone.

"Do you want to get drunk with me?"

She laughed. "Excuse me?"

"Sober, we know nothing. Drunk, maybe we'll drum up some absurd possibility."

The twitterpated teenaged girl in her heart stirred to life again. "If we get drunk, we might end up doing something we regret."

"If we stay sober, we might not do anything at all. I think I'd regret that more."

He stood so close that a tiny shift would put the soft skin of her cheek against the rough stubble of his five o'clock shadow. "Yeah. Okay. I'll have a drink with you."

His gaze moved from her eyes to her lips and lingered there. "I didn't ask you to have a drink. I asked you to get drunk."

The way the world tilted under her feet, she felt drunk already. She gave a tiny nod. He backed away, leaving a void between them. In for a penny, in for a pound. If she was going to give herself over to debauchery and bad choices, she may as well go the whole nine yards. "Not the lounge, though. Somewhere quieter."

When he smiled, she discovered that the rough and tough Gordon Westchester had dimples. At that moment, she realized the last time she'd fallen this hard for a guy, she ended up marrying him.

"How do you feel about Swedish models?" she asked.

"Too skinny. Too young. Too focused on hair."

Oh, man. She was in deep.

CHAPTER NINETEEN

Richard

RICHARD PRACTICALLY HAD TO JOG ACROSS THE LUXURIOUS lobby to keep up with Luca's long strides as he traveled through the ship. The younger man finally stopped at a swinging door in the back corner and glanced around. Richard ducked into a little forest of potted plants. His breath came in quick bursts. Maybe Burke had a point about the gym. Then again, too much exertion might kill a man his age. It might be better to save up his energy for moments such as these when he really needed it.

"Richard?"

He squeaked like a rubber chicken and spun around. "Whozit?"

Julia twisted her long strand of pearls around one finger. Her pointed red fingernail shone in the light of the crystal chandelier.

"Where are you running off to?"

His gaze darted to the swinging door through which Luca

had disappeared. "I...uh...had to use the little boy's room."

She raised an eyebrow. "In a potted plant?"

"What? No!"

She stepped closer.

He backed up and bumped into a palm tree.

"I like you a lot, Richard. You're strong and complicated. There's something inside you that's different from other men your age."

He swallowed, painfully aware that the lump in his throat wasn't the only thing getting hard. How humiliating! "I ain't nothing special."

She pressed her hand to his heart. "Oh, but you are special, Richard. I knew it from the moment I saw you."

A bead of sweat trickled down from his hairline. He swiped it away and tried to step left. She countered his move and blocked him. "Come back to my room, Richard."

All the blood in his brain rushed south, leaving him slightly dizzy. "That's not a good idea."

"I disagree. I think it's a fantastic idea."

Common sense poked its head out from a back corner of his mind, and he managed a halfway intelligent sentence, "I gotta go. There's something I need to do." Maybe, if he left right that instant, he'd be able to catch the dodgy waiter before he hurt anyone else.

Julia pressed closer. "Forget about the boy, Richard. He's not the one you want."

How did she know he was following the kid? His mind scrambled to fit the puzzle pieces together.

"He's not the killer." She watched him from beneath her lashes. "That's why you're chasing him, right? You think he might be the man behind the mysterious deaths aboard this ship?"

"The captain said they were natural deaths." He dodged right.

She moved with him. "The captain is a fool. You and I know the truth." One of the scary fingernails traced a pattern across the front of his shirt. The rough bark of the potted tree dug into his spine between his shoulder blades. Julia's curvy body pressed against his front side. She raised up on tiptoe until her lips hovered next to his ear. Her warm breath caused every hair on his body to stand on end. "You know because you're a hunter, right?" She giggled, a soft, girlish laugh, and whispered so softly he could barely make out the words, "And I know because I'm the monster that's killing people."

All the body parts that had so recently grown burning hot turned cold as ice, and he shivered under her touch.

"But you're a woman," he said.

"I noticed you noticing that. Walk me back to my room, Richard."

He shook his head.

Her hands moved between them and a little tickle forced an involuntary laugh from him.

"You're a woman," he said again. Terror pulsed through his veins, allowing no room for embarrassment over the pleading edge to his voice.

"Yes. Not a leszy, hunter. A leszachka."

She wiggled her fingers again, and he squirmed under the titillating torture. The bright blue and gold of the lobby grew dull and hazy around the edges. His muscles twitched and itched under her hands and then she stepped aside and he found his feet jerking forward, carrying him along in awkward halting motions. Julia walked behind him, one hand just above his left hip, right on the spot Barbara called his love handle. He snickered and snorted as he went. Tears burned his eyes.

Under her touch, he had no more control of himself than he would if he'd stuck a finger in a light socket.

A few folks passing by met his eye and grinned at the senile old man who couldn't stop laughing and moved on. He tried to say something, but he could no sooner speak than he could run. Somehow, she'd tied him to herself. She was leading him back to her room, and when they arrived, she was going to kill him.

The enormous ship suddenly seemed as tiny as a fishing boat, and in no time at all, they stood outside her door. She slipped her hand down a few inches. Richard's body twitched so hard he banged his head against the door frame.

"Careful, dear. We don't want the fun to end too quickly, now, do we?"

He laughed and gasped, tried to speak, and failed.

She produced a key card from Lord only knew where and passed it in front of the door latch. The green light flashed.

In a dim corner of his mind, he registered the sound of another door opening somewhere farther down the hall.

He summoned all his will and threw himself toward the floor. The leszachka caught him by the back of his neck and tossed him into the stateroom as if he weighed no more than a housecat. He landed hard, half on the bed and half off, uncertain of which half was pointed upward. Before he managed to sort it out, her hands were on him again, under his chin, moving along his sides, dancing across his inner thighs, and laughter racked his body with such force he wondered if his ribs would crack.

There wasn't a snowball's chance he could scramble away from her and make a run for the door. He did the only thing a man could do under the circumstances. He screamed like a teenage girl in a horror movie.

CHAPTER TWENTY

Burke

BURKE AND GORDON FOUND A TALL TABLE WITH TWO chairs on a high deck of the ship. He ordered a whiskey sour and she asked for a Manhattan.

He showed his dimples again. "I knew you'd be a whiskey woman."

"This seems like a whiskey occasion." She tapped her fingernail against the glass.

"Nervous?"

"Yes."

"Me too," he admitted.

"My husband left me. It took a really long time to figure out who I was without him."

"And now you're afraid to lose your identity as a strong, independent woman by tying yourself to another man."

She shrugged. "My mother says that's why he left me— because men don't enjoy strong, independent women."

"That's true, if they're insecure assholes."

She laughed and sipped her cocktail. The motion of the enormous ship on the smooth sea had a lulling effect. Now that the sun had set, the air had cooled to the exact temperature of her skin, wrapping her in a weird, pleasant, weightless feeling. The lights sparkled and reflected in the water. They might have been sailing through the stars. She took a deep breath and let some of the tension from their earlier adventure drain away. "This is good."

His gaze darted past her for a moment and then returned so quickly she might have imagined it. "Agreed."

"What about you? What tragic experience makes you nervous?"

He took a long drink and placed his glass back on the table with the gentleness one would show a baby bird. "I'm not a nice guy."

Burke believed him. "Not nice, maybe, but good."

"What do you base that on?"

"My gut," she said.

His laugh reminded her of distant thunder echoing off mountains. "Can I ask you something?" He looked past her again, but only for a second.

She resisted an urge to turn around and see what kept drawing his attention. "I don't promise an answer."

"Have you been fully honest with me about who you are?"

She finished her drink and ate the cherry. When she rubbed the stem between the tips of her forefingers, it twirled like a pinwheel. "I've been as honest as I feel I can be."

Music drifted upward from one of the lower decks, and for a while, they sat and listened in comfortable silence.

Gordon sat with his arms draped on the arms of the chair. It was a posture of relaxation, but something told her he'd be up and in motion in a split second if he had a reason to be.

"You know, when I came home from the Middle East, people said I had a certain look. They told me it looked like I had seen things that I could never unsee. My wife said I looked haunted."

"I suppose war does that to a person."

He tipped his head. "Yeah. I suppose it does. Thing is, though, she was wrong. I didn't feel haunted. I loved being a soldier. I was good at it. It was..." He turned his hand palm up as if hoping maybe the words he wanted would fall into it.

"It was a calling," she said.

The dimples again. "Yeah. Guess she didn't find that attractive. She left me for some jerk with an office on the top floor of a tall building."

"You're still trying to convince me you're not a nice guy?"

"No. I was just thinking. I never really knew exactly what they meant. I didn't understand what they saw that made them think that. I was just like everybody else. I dressed like a civilian. I ate like a civilian. I even forced myself to forget military-speak and talk like a civilian."

"You move through the world like a soldier," she said.

He raised a brow. "So do you. That's what made me think of it. I never knew what people saw that made them say those things until I met you. You look like you've seen things—the kind of things that, for other people, would make sleeping through the night impossible—and there is a part of you that loves it."

"There is a part of me that hates it. I see what my future holds."

"What's that?"

"My friend, Stanley, he..." Burke shook her head. "Everyone has a breaking point."

"Yeah. I suppose that's true." His eyes flicked to the side again. "Let's go somewhere else."

She didn't dare turn around. Something watched from behind her. "Where?"

"I'll walk you back to your room."

She bit her lip. "Gordon, I like you, but I'm not—"

"Just a friendly escort to the door," he said. "Unless you want me to come in."

Good Lord Almighty, yes, she wanted him to come in. That didn't make it a good idea, though. "All right," she conceded. "To the door, then."

He stayed at her side but never touched her as they walked along the deck, through the halls, and down the stairs. He never touched, but he was so close the heat from his skin burned her. By the time they reached the door, she was making a conscious effort not to breathe heavily like some sort of Neanderthal woman in heat.

She faced him. "I enjoyed this time."

He stepped closer, pressing her back against the wall. "Tell me to go away and I'll leave right now."

Not for all the money in the world. She put her palms against his chest and felt the flex of his muscles as he leaned in. His lips brushed hers so softly it might have just been his breath and—

"Burke! Thank God!" Stanley burst from his room.

Isaac let out a startled yelp. Apparently, he'd been coming down the hall just at that moment.

Gordon's body remained pressed against hers, but he swiveled his head in Stanley's direction.

Burke wondered if she could melt into a puddle and flow under the door.

"Why are you following us?" Gordon demanded.

"I'm not following you. I don't even know where you were," Stanley said.

Isabelle peeked out from Stanley's room.

Burke's jaw dropped open. "Stanley?"

"Not you," Gordon said. He stepped away from Burke and glared at Isaac. "You."

Isaac appeared to be on the verge of passing out. He mopped sweat from his forehead with the lacy cuff of his ruffled sleeve. "I..." He lifted his chin, squared his shoulders, and looked into Burke's eyes. "I love you. I've loved you from the first moment I met you, and I would be much better for you than this slab of mindless meat."

Gordon's lips pressed into a thin line.

"There's no time," Isabel cried, pulling on Stanley's sleeve. "He was screaming, screaming like a frightened child. Something terrible is happening."

"The leszy has your grandfather," Stanley told Burke.

Burke's gut twisted into a knot. "Where?"

"Show us," Stanley said to the girl at his side.

Her head whipped from side to side. "No. No way. Absolutely not. I'm out. I'm out of this scene. I'm out of this job. I'm off this ship, and I am never, ever stepping off land again."

"I need to know where!" Stanley held the girl by the front of her shirt.

Burke stepped between them. "Where's my grandfather?"

"In the Domina woman's cabin."

"I know where she lives," Gordon said. "Let's go." He took off at a sprint. Burke followed, Stanley keeping pace at her side. Isaac's platform heels thunked against the carpeted floor behind them.

They turned a corner and Gordon nearly ran over Captain Northrup. The captain didn't show any hint of surprise as the gang stumbled over their feet trying not to run over him. He reached into his jacket pocket and produced a gun. "I have cameras in my room, Westchester. I'm not the idiot you take me for."

"You kept a clear paper trail that can convict you. Obviously, you're not all that bright."

"We have to go," Stanley said.

Captain Northrup pointed the pistol at him. "No one goes until I say."

"You're a lunatic," Gordon said.

The captain's face turned an alarming shade of red. "I'm a freaking genius!"

"Go," Gordon said to Burke. "End of the hall. Staircase. First right, second left, door at the end of the hall. I'll handle this."

She looked from the gun to Gordon and back again.

"We have to go," Stanley said again.

"Go," Gordon told her.

"No!" The captain cocked the pistol.

Gordon grabbed his arm and forced it upward. A bullet lodged in the ceiling and white dust rained down. Gordon wrenched the man's arm and the gun clattered to the floor. He kicked it toward Burke.

Stanley took off running. Burke snatched up the weapon and followed, her heart pumping hard. She gritted her teeth and forced her mind into a state of clear, quiet calm. Gordon could take care of himself. Her grandfather needed her. She sent up a prayer, begging that they get there in time.

CHAPTER TWENTY-ONE

Richard

RICHARD'S LEFT ARM FLAILED IN AN ATTEMPT TO REACH HIS shoe.

The leszachka threw her head back and laughed.

Half an eternity, or maybe five minutes ago, she'd tossed him onto the bed. He'd landed flat on his back and she'd straddled him like a randy cowgirl. Her fingers never stopped moving over his body and his laughter had taken on a hoarse rasping edge. Pain radiated from beneath his breastbone in hot waves. Tears blurred his vision and every thought in his mind turned to static except one. *Stop. Dear God, please stop.*

Somewhere in the dark recesses of his consciousness, he knew if he could just reach his shoe he might be saved, but how could he with this monster in fancy lady skin pinning him down?

"You're still trying to fight? I knew you'd be magnificent. It's been ages since any of those geriatric old fools lasted this long. A twitch and a grunt and they're done."

He jerked away from her torturing right hand, but her left was there on the other side. Breath came in ragged, unsatisfying gasps, each shorter and more pathetic than the one before, and he realized this was how it would end for him.

Something slammed against the door.

The monster's hands stilled for one blessed moment.

The laugh on Richard's lips morphed into a sob.

Again, the door shuddered in its frame.

Julia growled as low and fierce as a lion.

Richard sucked in a real breath.

The door flew open and Stanley burst into the room, followed by at least two other people. Through his veil of tears, Richard saw Stanley's eyes grow wide, and he realized how the scene must appear. Oxygen and humiliation refueled his strength and he shoved the monster.

She slipped and fell, landing with a thud on the floor between the bed and the wall.

Richard lurched in the other direction and rolled off the bed. The impact knocked out what little breath he'd managed to catch.

Burke shouldered her way past Stanley and leveled a gun in Julia's direction. "Get up slow and keep your hands in the air."

Richard lay prone, staring up at Stanley and Burke. The other member of his rescue team remained hidden behind those two, but from the corner of his eye, he could make out a pair of purple suede high-heeled boots.

"That's right. Nice and easy. Keep those hands where I can see them," Burke said, from which Richard surmised that Julia must have been rising to her feet.

"How dare you treat me like this, interrupting my intimate time with my gentleman friend. I'm disgusted."

"Put those hands back up," Burke shouted.

Julia laughed. The sound sent chills up Richard's spine and instinct sent him rolling to his hands and knees so he could crawl to safety. He clambered around behind the little group of saviors and propped his back against the wall. His lungs pumped air in and out of his body in great heaving gasps.

"Your gun can't hurt me, girl."

"It won't help you," she said.

Richard's thoughts surged and faded in the same way as his breath. He fought to latch on to any of them. Stars danced and flashed on the edges of his vision. It seemed important to take off his shoes, so he did, but then he couldn't remember why.

"Let me go," Julia said. "If you let me go, I'll disappear. If you insist on having this fight, I will kill every one of you."

Richard looked down at the shoe in his hand. Why was he holding his shoe?

Burke scoffed. "You've got to be kidding."

"I don't like you. You meddle. You're cocky. You need to learn your place," Julia declared.

Isaac pushed his way into the room. "Hey! You can't talk to her that way!"

"Oh, shut up, you little fairy." She snatched the lamp off the nightstand and whipped it at Isaac.

Burke threw herself sideways and knocked him out of the way, taking the blow herself. The lamp hit the side of her head. Isaac crashed into the door frame and they both fell to the floor next to Richard. The little man lay still as death. Burke tried to say something, but though her lips moved, no sound came out. Blood dripped from her temple onto the carpet. Her eyes rolled up so only the whites showed.

"Not another move," Gordon shouted from the doorway.

Julia leaped onto the bed and springboarded into Gordon. He fell onto the heap of bodies by the door and his gun clattered away.

The monster had Richard again. She lifted him by the shirt and dragged him down the hall.

He flapped his arms like a startled chicken, but it had all the effect of a butterfly pushing an elephant. Panic erupted from his core. He didn't want to die. Not like this. He sought out salvation and his gaze landed on Stanley.

Thin, shaky, old Stanley, so pathetic, the monster didn't bother to take notice of him. His eyes were wide, his cheeks wet with tears, but in the last fraction of a second, before the creature tossed Richard into a room where the door had been propped open, something changed.

Stanley's eyes narrowed. His spine straightened. His shoulders squared.

Julia slammed the door shut and threw the deadbolt. "I'll finish what I started with you and then I'll take them, and then maybe I'll eat every person on this ship. I can change and get away and not one soul will be any wiser. I'm tired of being this old lady, anyway."

She crawled onto the bed and slung one leg over him, her hand tracing a path over the round paunch of his belly. Richard gasp/laugh/sobbed. "Maybe I'll become your granddaughter, Richard. She's a bitch, but she's undeniably beautiful. I could really go places with a body like that."

Three shots rang out in quick succession and the door banged open. Stanley crossed the room in two long strides and swung his arm in a wide arc. Light flashed off a silver blade and a spray of something warm and wet hit Richard's face. He blinked and cringed away from it, and opened his eyes just in time to see Julia's head tip left and roll from her neck. Her body fell forward onto him. He shoved it away. Her torso hit the floor with a thud, and Richard lay on the bed, drenched in gore, staring up at the twinkling eyes of the hunter who stood over him. A little grin touched the corner of Stanley's mouth. "I'm feeling much better."

CHAPTER TWENTY-TWO

Burke

BURKE'S EYES FLUTTERED OPEN AND SHE SQUINTED AGAINST the light, dim though it was. A dull throbbing pulse pounded in her skull. A semi-circle of concerned male faces hovered over her. Her grandfather and Stanley, Gordon and Ike. A pastel-striped curtain isolated them from the rest of the room.

"Welcome back, kid," Richard said. "You had me nervous as a long-tailed cat in a room full of rocking chairs there for a while."

"Sorry about that," she said. Speaking increased the tempo of the drumbeat inside her head. She closed her eyes and waited for the throbbing to settle down. When she had mastered it to some degree, she looked at Stanley.

The old hunter stood straight and tall. He held his hands one atop the other on the brass handle of his cane. His baggy suit was pressed and clean. The wrinkles around the corners of his eyes scrunched upward.

"You're okay?" she asked.

He took a deep breath. "Yes. I believe I am. Thank you."

Tears burned her eyes. She had to look away or the immensity of her relief would send her into hysterics, and sobbing at that moment might just make her aching head explode.

Gordon stood at the left side of the bed.

"Not a great first date," she said.

"Not my worst."

She laughed. It hurt almost as bad as she'd expected crying would.

Ike stepped forward with a shell full of seawater. "Here. This should help." He dipped his finger in the water and drew a line across her forehead.

The pain subsided to a manageable level.

"You'll be all better soon. You're nearly as strong as Stanley."

She thanked him and tried to organize her thoughts. They'd been running toward Julia's room to help Richard, and then Julia had thrown a lamp, and...

"Where's Isaac?"

Ike stepped aside and tugged on the curtain that encircled her bed. Isaac lay in a nearby bed, snoring quietly.

Relief cooled the rush of adrenaline. "What happened?"

Richard explained about suspecting Luca and being cornered by Julia. He told how Julia'd revealed herself and then forced him back to her room. "If you and Stan hadn't shown up, I'd a been as screwed as a portside whore."

She looked at Stanley, who stood there listening, as dapper and alert as she'd ever seen him. "How?"

"It was the girl, Isabelle. She'd been helping a friend who wasn't feeling well—performing turn-down service in the part of the ship where Julia had been staying—when she heard

Dick call for help. She was already suspicious. The whole crew's been nervous—"

"You have no idea the rumors that were flying," Ike said.

Stanley went on, "She was actually trying to find you. The poor child pounded on your door like she was trying to break it down, but of course, you weren't there. I'd only just returned from dinner and I stuck my head out to see what was happening. When she said Richard was in trouble…" He gave a little self-deprecating shrug. "It was as if she ran a magnet over the shrapnel of those scattered thoughts I'd been unable to manage on my own since the incident with the leprechaun—"

Ike gasped and they all turned to him.

"You fought a leprechaun and lived to tell about it?"

"We fought *with* a leprechaun, and I only survived because of his intervention," Stanley said.

Ike's massive form swayed slightly. "You're so brave."

"There's a fine line between bravery and a lack of good sense," Stanley replied. "At any rate, as soon as I knew Dick was in trouble, I knew I had to help. I was headed that way when I heard you in the hall and, well, you know the rest."

Burke reached out for Richard's hand and he gave her fingers a gentle squeeze.

"I'm glad you're okay, Grandpa."

"Back at you, kid."

Jerry Lee Lewis started singing "Great Balls of Fire" and they all looked around for the source of the music.

"I think it's coming from your pocket," Gordon told Richard.

Richard produced his phone and stared at it like he'd never seen the device before. He poked the screen and held it to his ear. "This is Richard. Hold on." He moved the phone away from his ear, fiddled with his hearing aid, and put it back again.

As he listened, his brows drew into a scowl. "I see... No, no, she's fine. She's here, right next to me... Yes. I understand. I'll let her know. All right then, thanks to you. Keep us posted if you hear anything else. Right. All right, then. Yeah. I'll let you know." He held the device at arm's length and poked it once more before slipping it back into his pocket. "Nathanial," he said, looking at Burke.

"I called him to let him know about Greg."

Richard pushed his dentures around with his tongue.

"Oh, the suspense," Stanley said, a little grin on his lips.

Burke's heart soared to see him so playful.

"The jerk showed up. Introduced himself around town. Annoyed enough people that they remembered him, and then he disappeared," Richard said.

Burke's heart skipped a beat. "You mean, he left."

Richard held her gaze. "Disappeared. His car's still there. Left his stuff in the cabin at the campground, cellphone, wallet, and all."

"Who's Greg?" Gordon asked.

"My ex-husband," Burke said.

"The one with the underwear model?"

"Yeah, well, not anymore. He was running from a witch—"

Ike gasped and she looked at him.

"Sorry." He fanned himself with his hand. "You keep talking about witches and, frankly, witches terrify me. There's a sea witch that lords over the merpeople—Ursula—and she's just awful. You wouldn't believe the things she's done."

The voice of The Little Mermaid sang in her mind and Burke had to struggle to remember her train of thought. The ache in her head was increasing again. "He was afraid he was being followed."

"It sounds like he was right," Stanley said.

Richard harrumphed. "We could leave it alone. It's not like he don't deserve whatever he gets."

Burke took a deep breath. "Let's talk about it later."

They all grew annoyingly accommodating, and the four of them fussed over her like a gaggle of mother geese until she pretended to be asleep and they tiptoed from the room.

She lay on the narrow hospital bed with her eyes closed and tried to sort through her feelings—elation over Stanley's recovery, relief about her grandfather's safety, dread regarding what might have happened to Greg. By the time she drifted away to sleep, she knew what they had to do, and she knew she didn't want to do it.

CHAPTER TWENTY-THREE

Gordon

GORDON KNOCKED ON THE DOOR OF BURKE'S STATEROOM and hoped to God neither of the old guys would stick out their head to see who was there. Ever since she'd left the infirmary, they'd hovered over the girl like she was an infant. It wasn't an ideal situation for a man trying to...

What exactly was he trying to do?

He barely knew the woman, but he knew enough to know he wanted to know more about her.

He knew enough to know that it wasn't every day a female could tie his thoughts in a knot.

She opened the door. Her jeans and tee-shirt looked just as good on her as the fancy dresses he'd seen her wear. Tiny diamond studs sparkled on her earlobes. He wondered if she'd enjoy a gentle nibble there.

"May I come in for a minute?"

She hesitated, but stepped back and let him pass by.

The click of the door latching made him nervous as a

schoolboy. He laughed and admitted as much to her. It must have been the right thing to do because she leaned back against the door and smiled at him.

"It was a shame our evening ended the way it did," she said.

"Yeah. I thought maybe I could beg the chance to wrap things up properly with you."

She cocked her head. "I'm not sure I know what you mean."

He advanced slowly, gave her plenty of time to tell him to bugger off, but she stayed still as a statue until he stood so close the heat of her body seeped into the fabric of his clothes and, at last, he held her in his arms. Her mouth tasted of peppermint. Her skin was silk over the firm muscles that stretched and flexed as she wrapped her arms around him.

After too short a time, she pulled away. With one long, slim finger, she traced the line of his jaw. "I don't understand."

"Don't understand what?" He gave thanks that his voice didn't squeak like an adolescent boy's.

"Why we need to wrap things up."

He leaned closer, pressing her strong body against the door. "You'll stay? Sail the seven seas and be my pirate wench?"

Her smile faded. "I can't do that."

He'd expected as much, but she threw him for a loop when she added, "But you could come with us."

"Where?"

She leaned in and kissed him again, ran her fingers through his hair and down the sides of his neck to his shoulders, then she gently pushed him away.

He stepped back, breathless.

"Let's talk," she murmured.

Talk. Right. She wanted to talk. Talking was good. "Okay, then."

Her gaze flicked to the bed. "Maybe not here, though. You make it hard for me to concentrate."

He laughed. "The feeling is mutual."

She slipped her hand into his and they walked together through the halls to the library and settled into side-by-side armchairs. Sitting with her felt as natural as breathing. The room was cool and quiet and deserted, as always, and he wondered why more people didn't take advantage of the space. It was maybe the prettiest place on the whole ship.

Burke said, "So, my secret's out."

"Yup. I know now you're a liar."

She didn't laugh as he'd hoped, but nodded. "I'm a liar and a criminal. Stanley, my grandfather, me, we break the law pretty much every day."

"Sometimes, the ends justify the means," he said.

"Yeah. That's what I tell myself, but at the same time, I'm always aware that's a slippery slope to travel. Our lives are complicated, Gordon. What we do is dangerous and messy. There's no glory in it, and even less pay."

"But you're saving people."

"We are, yes."

He realized then that he was a little jealous of what they had. The sparkle in her eyes, the power she exuded when she walked—it all came from knowing who you were and why you lived, and it was sexy as hell. Who was he? A security guard? Why did he live? To file reports about forgotten earrings and lost purses? Burke's reality was wilder and more vast than average folks could even conceive. A hunger to know the truth clawed at his gut. "Tell me what you've seen."

She laughed. "I don't have that much time."

"Tell me a bit."

"My first hunt was a hidebehind. They're shapeshifters that

live in the forest. That was less than a year ago. The three of us killed a shapeshifter. It was the monster who'd murdered my grandmother, though at the time she died, my grandfather had no idea about any of this. Oh, and I fought The Devil." She rolled her eyes upward and thought for a few seconds. "Well...I didn't fight her, exactly. I trapped her once, temporarily, and I tricked her."

"So, The Devil is real and he's a she?"

Burke nodded. "Everything is real."

"Everything?"

"Well, no. I mean, probably not everything, and some things are extinct now, but yeah, mostly. And hunting is... You were a soldier, right? You know how it is. There's adrenaline and strength and purpose, but sometimes you see certain things that just never leave you."

"Is that what happened to Stanley?"

Her gaze grew distant and sad. "What happened to Stanley was my fault. He told me to be careful. He warned me to stay in a safe place and I didn't listen. They came to rescue me and he..." She shuddered.

"I didn't mean to make you sad."

"Stanley was saved by a leprechaun." She grinned, waiting for his reaction.

He remembered someone bringing up leprechauns in the infirmary, but he'd still been trying to process a tickle monster disguised as a rich old woman. "Little green guy?"

"He wasn't green. Not all that little either, really. He blended pretty well."

"Does he live at the end of the rainbow?" Gordon asked.

"I'm not sure. I think he has an apartment in New York."

Gordon grinned. He knew full well that he looked like a

love-sick fool and didn't care. "I have never met a woman like you."

"That's probably true," she said. "I meant what I said. You could come with us."

"You never told me where."

"Does it matter?" she asked.

"Not really," he said.

She tapped her nails against the upholstered arm of the chair. "We're going to New Mexico. My ex is in trouble, maybe dead. Our best guess is that he was being hunted by a witch, but I've got to be honest, that was our best guess on this ship, too. Seems like we put everything on the witches' shoulders whether they deserve it or not."

"And if it is a witch and you find her?"

Burke held his gaze.

"Right. Sorry." Restlessness blossomed in him and he had to get out of the chair before he burst. He paced to the bookshelf and idly glanced at the titles there, not really paying attention to any of them. Memories flashed across his mind. He was in a foxhole, listening to his friend's dying wishes and feeling a little jealous of how many goodbyes the man wanted to say. Gordon had no one to mourn him when he left this world.

He was slamming both feet against the brake pedal of a Jeep, trying not to drive into the wreckage of the vehicle that had just exploded in front of him. He was wrestling a terrorist to the ground to slap handcuffs on him and swearing if he ever got out of the god-forsaken Middle East, he'd find the cushiest job in America. He'd succeeded. It was awful.

Burke watched him as if she had all the time in the world. With her arms resting on the arms of the chair and her long legs crossed, she looked like a queen holding court. "We don't have a home," she said. "When we decide to leave New Mexico, it'll be to chase something else. We hunt monsters one after another. There are thousands of them, millions maybe. We'll never be done. This is how we'll die."

He leaned back against the shelf. "I'll come, but I need to finish things up here first. Northrup needs to be put away. I've got obligations, but the second they're done, I'll come."

She smiled and her sparkling brown eyes scrunched up at the corners, but as they walked back to her cabin, he couldn't shake the feeling that she didn't fully believe he'd stick to his word. No matter. In time, she'd believe in him. In them. For the moment, he would believe enough for both of them, which was funny, because a week earlier, he never would have dreamed he'd fall in love.

CHAPTER TWENTY-FOUR

Richard

RICHARD HOPED HIS PANTS WOULDN'T SPLIT. THEY'D FIT fine five days earlier. He hadn't eaten that much. The cooks on the ship must lace the food with extra calories or something. He had to admit, some of the grub hadn't been half bad, but he found himself looking forward to getting some Kentucky Fried Chicken on the way out of town. He'd woken up with a hankering for it.

One last check of the room confirmed that he'd gathered all his belongings. He zipped the duffle bag and stepped into the hall at the same moment as Stanley.

Stanley wore a white fedora tipped forward on his bald head. His waistcoat hugged his slim torso. The crease in his pants would have made Luca look like a slob. Richard could see his own reflection in the man's shoes.

"Your clothes fit," Richard said.

"I find it makes movement easier," Stanley replied.

Richard scowled. "Yesterday, you was too skinny and your clothes hung on you like an old scarecrow."

"They have some fine shops aboard this ship, Dick. I noticed you found some new shoes in one of them, as well."

"You coulda bought clothes after we got off the boat for half the price."

"Life is too short to worry about nickels and dimes, my friend."

Richard harrumphed. Easy to say when you've always had an abundance of nickels and dimes. He banged on Burke's door.

"She already left. Said she'd meet us in the lobby. I think she wanted a few minutes alone with Mr. Westchester."

"She tell you she invited him to hunt with us?" Richard asked. When Burke had dropped that bomb on him the night before, he'd been as shocked as a cowboy peeing on an electric fence. What did they need one more for? He didn't put up too much of a fight since the guy wasn't coming right away, but darned if he was gonna ride around the countryside hunting monsters with a busload of tourists in tow.

Stanley confirmed that he'd already heard the news.

"And what do you think of that?" Richard asked.

"I think a hunter will always be led to the hunt, and those who are not meant to be involved will drift away to their familiar world."

"So, you approve or not?"

"I don't think my approval or lack thereof matters in the slightest."

"That girl don't need her heart broken again."

Stanley grinned. "I'm more worried for Gordon. The poor man thinks he knows her and her work."

Richard harrumphed again and hitched his bag up onto his shoulder.

The girl Isabelle waited at the end of the hall, helping guests with last minute needs and saying her goodbyes to everyone.

"I owe you a debt," Richard told her.

Her smile was pretty as a summer day. "I'm glad you are safe."

"You staying on the boat?"

"Oh, God no! I'm going home. I'll find another way to travel the world. This is not my calling."

Richard knew exactly what she meant.

They made it all the way to the lobby before bumping into Ike. The god of the sea fanned his face as Stanley approached. "You looked fabulous before. Now, you take my breath away. Are you sure you won't stay?"

"You flatter an old man," Stanley said. "Thank you for your help."

Ike extended a hand. "It is an honor to know you, hunter. I'm glad you are well."

Burke and Gordon walked with them down the gangplank. The lovers whispered goodbyes and exchanged kisses while Richard and Stanley stood by like a couple of rubes, and then they passed through customs and back into the regular good ol' U S of A.

When they opened the doors of the convertible, heat waves rolled out. Stanley lowered the top and they all climbed in. Stanley sat in the driver's seat and seeing him there brought a smile to Richard's face.

"You look downright happy," Stanley told him.

Richard switched on the oldies station. "It's good to be home."

SNEAK PEEK AT SOME LOVES NEVER DIE

Monsters and Mayhem Book Four

CHAPTER ONE

Richard

Outside of the storybook cabin snugged away in the Sangre de Cristo Mountains near Santa Fe, New Mexico, fat snowflakes drifted down from heavy gray clouds like the feathers of falling angels. Inside, a fire crackled and popped and saturated the air with its fragrant heat.

Richard dipped a tarnished silver spoon into a bowl of green chili stew and came up with a thick chunk of pork and a good amount of broth. On that cold winter day, the flavors burst across his tongue the way the warm desert sun bursts across the mesa in June. He understood the importance of cherishing the best moments of being human. After all, if he'd learned anything in the year since he became a hunter of supernatural evil, it was that death was the least of a man's worries. Death came for everyone. It was only natural. When unnatural things happened to you, *that's* when you needed to worry.

To Richard's left, his granddaughter, Burke, tore off bits of a homemade flour tortilla and popped each piece into her mouth. She was worried about Greg, her idiot ex-husband, and she was right to be worried. At the moment, her big brown eyes were focused on Stan Kapcheck.

Everyone's eyes were always on friggin' Stan Kapcheck with his stylish leather boots and his well-pressed flannel shirt. What kind of a weirdo took a clothes iron to flannel, anyway?

Richard's eyes burned. He blinked hard. Dang, if he wasn't just as happy as a tornado in a trailer park to have that annoying old peacock whole and healthy again. They'd come all too close to losing Stanley in recent times, and Richard couldn't quite wrap his mind around the idea of life without him, even if he was sometimes as annoying as a mosquito in your underpants.

Stanley sat to Richard's right. He studied the map of the Santa Fe area that lay in the center of the rustic wooden table. "So, we know that Greg was headed for Tesuque, which is due north of town, off of eighty-four, but you say you have it on good authority that he was seen southwest of here, in Agua Fria."

Their host, Nathanial, occupied the final chair at the table, directly across from Richard. Nathanial scratched his bushy, chest-length beard, knocking one of the pink plastic butterfly clips askew. "Not only Agua Fria. He touched base in Chupadero, Cañada de los Alamos, Las Dos—all the way south to Clines Corners. He found ins with the communities, and I mean all of them—the Wiccans, the natives, the Catholics. He spent three days at that nudist spa downtown."

Burke snorted.

Richard scowled. Thinking about his granddaughter's ex-husband with his junk hanging out was enough to kill a healthy man's appetite.

Almost.

He scooted his chair back and went to the wood-burning stove to help himself to seconds.

"He wasn't hard to track at first," Nathanial said. "Cast a simple spell and bam!"

Richard jumped and almost slopped his stew all over the floor. He kept his words to himself, though. It didn't seem polite to scold the hand that fed you.

"Bam, what?" Burke asked.

"Bam, he disappeared. He was there. Then he wasn't." Nathanial's cat, Jeremiah, leaped onto his owner's immense lap and helped himself to a few licks of the man's stew. "I widened the search to all New Mexico, North America, the world. Now, y'all know that the wider it goes, the less accurate it gets, but still...there should have been something."

Burke pushed her food aside, half-eaten. "So, he's dead?"

Stanley ran a hand over his shiny bald head. "Not necessarily. Nathanial, you told us earlier that there was a disturbance of some sort, right about the time Greg disappeared. Do you think there's a connection?"

"Sure I don't know," the big man answered while scratching his cat's head. "I know two things happened. Don't know if they're connected."

"What kind of disturbance? I ain't real clear on what you meant by that," Richard said around a mouthful of green chilis.

"The kind that makes magical folk wake up in the night, sick to their stomach. Something's off. Bad mojo. Energy gone wrong. Poor feng shui. Does that make it clearer?"

"'Bout as clear as barnwood."

Burke tapped her nails against the table. The cat watched the dance of pink enameled surfaces with a twitching tail. A loud crack from the fire shifted the logs, sending a volcano of red sparks into the chimney.

"I bedded an aboriginal dream walker once," Nathanial said.

They all stared at him, even the cat.

Nathanial shrugged a hamhock of a shoulder. "I only bring it up because the poor woman turned out to be as crazy as a loon. She ended up being taken into state custody and, so far as I know, she continues to live out her days weaving macramé under close supervision."

"I'm sure it wasn't your fault," Stanley said.

Richard shook his head and ate his soup. A year earlier, he'd been wasting away at Everest Senior Living, hanging around waiting for Death to come calling as it did for men his age. Turns out he didn't die there. Stanley saved his wrinkled old butt from soul-eating monsters pretending to be nurses, and in the months since then, he'd crisscrossed the lower forty-eight and seen more weird than most people ever dreamed of. That said, the humans out-weirded the monsters on a consistent basis.

"It might have been my fault," Nathanial said, sounding fairly unconcerned with the idea of driving a woman to madness. "I only bring it up because I think that's where you should start."

Burke's fingers stilled. "With your ex-lover?"

Great, rolling guffaws bellowed from Nathanial. He slapped the table, sending the cat racing for safety in some quieter part of the house. "No, no. She wouldn't be able to tell you anything useful unless your man is in another plane of existence."

"He's *not* my man," Burke said through gritted teeth.

Nathanial went on as though she hadn't spoken. "I think your best lead is Kenneth. He's an orderly at the Villa Cierto Health Care Center for Seniors. He's special."

Stanley polished off his dinner and dabbed at the corners of his mouth. "Would you mind terribly being a bit more specific?"

"Okay."

Burke met her grandfather's gaze and rolled her eyes. Richard felt her pain. Listening to the other two men was like trying to make sense out of squirrel chatter.

"About the current topic of conversation, please," Stanley said.

"Oh, sure. Kenneth is from the Acoma Pueblo. He wears a lot of turquoise jewelry. He's employed as an orderly, but his real job is keeping the spirits quiet. He's successful more often than not."

Richard leaned forward. "What spirits?"

"All the spirits," Nathanial said.

"In the world?" Burke asked.

Laughter returned—a rolling earthquake of merriment. "Oh, no. No, no, no. That's funny!" He waved a hand the size of a dinner plate in front of his whiskered face and then slapped his knee several times in quick succession. After a few deep breaths he said, "Villa Cierto is haunted, of course. It was built on the site of the former graveyard used by the penitentiary and it—"

Richard nearly spit his dentures out. "What in the Sam Hill was any fool thinking, building a dang nursing home on top of a graveyard?"

"The land was inexpensive, I imagine," Nathanial said.

"My God, it must be the most haunted building in the Southwest," Burke said.

Nathanial snorted. "You serious? You haven't spent much time in Santa Fe, have you? Anyway, Villa Cierto ain't so bad. Good old Kenneth keeps things in check."

"And you believe he would know where Greg is?" Stanley asked.

"He's as good a guy as any to ask. He's got more eyes in this town than a seraph, and he knows people who know magic far beyond my own."

"By eyes, do you mean monsters?" Burke asked.

"Just people, so far as I know," Nathanial said.

"You got some pretty good magic," Richard said, thinking of the marvelous healing balm the strange man had given them. The smelly stuff had been a literal lifesaver in the past, not only soothing aching bones and joints, but healing a stab wound to Stanley's heart with miraculous speed.

Nathanial stood and began clearing their plates. "Just parlor tricks, compared to some."

Burke tugged the map toward her side of the table. "Okay. So, tomorrow morning we go into town and talk to this man, Kenneth. I'd go tonight, but I'm not sure we can get off this mountain in the dark with the snow coming down like this. We shouldn't waste time, though. If Greg's off the grid in a spiritual sense... I mean...that could mean anything, right? It could be like what happened to Stanley or me."

Richard shuddered. It had been a rough few months. Burke's mother had set her up with a loser who ended up sending a demon from a shadow realm to possess her and make her obey him and, in the rescuing, Stanley lost a piece of himself that left him so wounded none of them were certain he'd recover until only a week or so ago. If his ex-grandson-in-law was in that kind of trouble then Burke was right to worry.

"Why do you want so badly to save not-your-man?" Nathanial asked from his place by the sink.

Jeremiah the cat poked his head around the corner as if curious to know the answer to that question.

Burke wrapped her arms around herself. Her gaze wandered from the fireplace, to the rough-hewn beams in the ceiling, and finally landed on Richard. "I was led to this hunt. It's not my place to judge who deserves saving. My job is to stand in the gap between humanity and whatever wants to destroy it."

Pride thumped through Richard's veins with every beat of his feeble old heart. The kid never ceased to amaze him. From her, he was learning about what kind of person he wanted to be.

"Very well, then, it's settled," Stanley said. "In the morning, we hunt at the retirement home."

His words brought the reality of the situation sailing into Richard's gut like a well-placed Kung-fu kick. "Hold on."

"Something wrong, Dick?" Stanley asked.

Richard scowled. Lord, but he hated being called Dick and that old fart knew it, too. "You listen to me, Stan Kapcheck. The Devil Herself is gonna be ice skating in Hell before I set foot inside a haunted retirement home." The very thought of wandering around inside a place like that turned his bowels to water. "I got locked up in an old folk's home, and I sat there waiting for death and, by golly, death darn near found me there."

"Grandpa, you weren't locked up," Burke said.

He smacked his hand on the table. "You don't know how it was. If I never go back in any kind of old folk's home again that'll be too soon, let alone one built on a friggin' prison graveyard."

"You're not scared are you?" Stanley asked. A grin tipped one corner of his mouth northward.

Burke reached over and took her grandfather's hand. "Don't tease, Stanley. Aren't you the one who taught us that wise men listen to their fear, but are never ruled by it? Grandpa will help us. He'll come through. He does, every time."

Richard swallowed the lump in his throat and squeezed the kid's hand.

Nathanial stumped over to a shelf, retrieved a fat book, and dropped it on the table.

"What's this?" Burke asked. "A spell book?"

The big man dried his hands on his yellow daisy-print apron. "No, but spelling's important. It's all in alphabetical order. Phone book. Cell service is spotty, at best, in these parts. You might need some good old-fashioned paper sources to find names and addresses." He jerked his hairy chin in Richard's direction. "Maybe he's got a point about the retirement home. Sniff out the trail. See what's to see."

"You could come with us, you know," Stanley said.

Nathanial's eyes grew wide and then he started laughing again. His laughter reverberated off the walls of the house. Tears poured out of his eyes and disappeared into the tangle of growth on his face. He shook his head, turned his back, and disappeared down the hall, laughing all the while. A door clicked shut and muffled the sound.

The three hunters of all things supernatural looked at each other.

After a moment, the creak of a door opening reached their ears. "Towels in the closet. Sleep anywhere you like, but not on the big canopy bed. That one's Jeremiah's and he'll claw your eyes out if you lay in it." The door clicked shut again and they were left to find their own way to their beds.

OTHER BOOKS IN THE MONSTERS AND MAYHEM SERIES

Some Monsters Never Die

Some Legends Never Die

Some Sailors Never Die

Coming Soon

Some Loves Never Die